**A man with a plan. . .**

"Upon the morrow, Higgins, I shall require you to carry out a few errands. I need a wardrobe suitable for a lady of, say, seventy years."

"According to what measurements, sir?"

"My own, you nodcock! Who else would I be purchasing clothing for? Furthermore, I shall need undergarments, and—" Heedless of his stunned servant, Sir Harry made a vague gesture in the direction of his chest. "—Something to fill 'em up with. Also a wig, one of those powdered things like old Lady Letton wears. I've no idea where one buys them, but I'm sure they must be available somewhere. You shall make inquiries."

"Yes, sir," said Higgins in faltering tones.

"But be discreet, mind you!"

"I shouldn't dream of being otherwise," vowed his servant, reflecting that his young master had gone round the bend, just like the poor old King. "Will there be anything else, sir?"

"Just one more thing." Turning toward the looking glass, Sir Harry studied his reflection for a long moment until his image faded and disappeared, replaced with the less pleasant picture of Olivia waltzing by in the marquess of Mannerly's arms. Stroking his sidewhiskers almost lovingly, he commanded, "Shave 'em off, Higgins."

**"A light and lively romp written with humor and grace."**
***—Romance Communications***

# Miss Darby's Duenna

Sheri Cobb South

PrinnyWorld Press

MISS DARBY'S DUENNA



**Publisher's Cataloging-in-Publication**
***(Provided by Quality Books, Inc.)***

South, Sheri Cobb
Miss Darby's duenna / Sheri Cobb South – 1st ed.
p. cm.
LCCN: 99-93288
ISBN: 0-9668005-1-6

1. Regency--England--London--Fiction.
2. London (England)--Fiction. 3. Female impersonators--England--Fiction. 4. Marriages of royalty and nobility--England--Fiction.
I. Title.

PS3569.O74M57 1999 813'.54
QBI99-969

First printing, 1999.
For information on this or other PrinnyWorld Press titles, contact:

PrinnyWorld Press
P. O. Box 248
Saraland, AL 36571
http://members.aol.com/PrinnyWrld/intro.html

To the 300 “Heyerites” of the
Georgette Heyer Internet Listservice,
with thanks for their unwavering support.

# Miss Darby's Duenna

## 1

When there is so much love on one side, there is no occasion for it on the other.
JANE AUSTEN, *Juvenilia*

Sir Harry Hawthorne, a strapping young gentleman of some four-and-twenty years, was a man with a purpose. He had been bred to this purpose for most of his life, and now in preparation for the execution of his mission, he guided his roan gelding down the country lane linking his ancestral home with Darby House, its nearest neighbor. He had every expectation of success in his undertaking, for besides being blessed with an optimistic nature, he was a young man of considerable wealth and social standing in rural Leicestershire. Besides being the holder of a baronetcy, he possessed the added charms of a headful of stylishly cropped sandy hair, a pair of speaking hazel eyes, and a firm square jaw enhanced by a fine pair of sidewhiskers of which he was inordinately proud. His cutaway coat of Devonshire brown, biscuit-colored buckskin breeches, and white-topped riding boots all proclaimed him the epitome of the fashionable country gentleman.

Not that Sir Harry was a rustic, by any stretch of the imagination. On the contrary, he much preferred the gaieties of town life to the tranquility of the country, and fancied himself, one minor contretemps notwithstanding, one of Society's most dashing ornaments. Until his father's death some twelve months previously had recalled him to the bosom of his family, he could usually be found in London, blowing a cloud at White's, stripping with his cronies at Gentleman Jackson's, or ogling actresses from the pit at Covent Garden. Recalling these pleasant pastimes from which he had been too long absent, he urged his horse onward, impatient to complete his mission so that he might return to the metropolis and resume his chosen way of life.

It was not until he entered the gates of Darby House that he began to waver in his purpose; after all, this was not something he did every day. As horse and rider made their way up the raked gravel drive which led to the house, Sir Harry frowned thoughtfully into the distance at the barren trees which made up his own Home Wood. Perhaps he should have brought flowers; it was his observation that females set great store by such things. The roses in his gardens had not yet begun to bloom, but he was sure the hothouses at Hawthorne Grange would have yielded something worthy of the occasion. Yes, he should have brought flowers. But now the edifice that was Darby House loomed before him, and it was too late to remedy the omission.

He surrendered his roan to Colonel Darby's groom, who had been watching for his arrival, and then, mounting the steps two at a time, reached for the door knocker. Before his hand touched the polished brass knocker, the heavy double doors parted before him, and the butler, who had known Sir Harry since he was in short coats, informed him rather grandly that Miss Darby awaited him in the Blue Saloon. Everyone, it seemed, was aware of his mission. Dismissing the butler with a nod, he made his way to this sanctum with the ease of long familiarity with the house and its residents, pausing midway up the stairs to provide himself with a floral offering from a large urn on the landing.

Upon reaching the Blue Saloon, he paused uncertainly before the open door. Beyond it sat Miss Olivia Darby, a solitary figure dressed in a simple round gown of blue muslin, a matching ribbon threaded through her dusky curls. Her gloved hands were clenched tightly in her lap in silent testimony to her unique rôle in his mission. Sir Harry took off his curly-brimmed beaver and raked his fingers through his sandy hair, disarranging his fashionable crop.

"Hullo, Livvy," he said at last, taking two uncertain steps into the room. "I suppose you know why I am here."

Her tremulous smile informed him that his surmise was correct. "I daresay I can guess. Mama told me you had something particular to ask."

The look of relief on Sir Harry's face was unmistakable. He strode forward with something approaching his earlier confidence and grinned down at her. "Well then, Livvy, what is it to be? Will you do me the honor of becoming my wife?"

A more observant gentleman than Sir Harry might have noted the spectrum of emotions which washed over Miss Darby's expressive countenance upon the receipt of this declaration. Anticipation gave way to confusion, and confusion ever so briefly to pain, before every trace of emotion was replaced with the delicate arching of her left eyebrow in a look of ironic amusement. But alas, observant poor Sir Harry was not, and he heard only her faintly mocking reply.

"But, Harry, this is so sudden!"

"Dash it, Livvy, how can you say it's sudden when you just told me you were expecting it?" he demanded impatiently. "Always knew I'd offer for you as soon as I finished at Oxford; known it since we were in leading strings!"

Miss Darby weighed this declaration, and found it wanting. "Does my memory fail me, Harry, or has it been nigh on three years since you finished at Oxford?"

Sir Harry crumpled the brim of his hat in his hands. This was not going at all as he had expected. "Well, Livvy, no sense in rushing into things. I mean, a fellow likes to see a bit of the world before tying himself down, y'know."

"I'm beginning to," Miss Darby said with a sigh. "And what of me,

Harry? Should I not have the opportunity to 'see a bit of the world' before tying myself down, as well? Mama wishes to take me to London this spring, so that I might make my come-out before we—that is, before any sort of announcement is made."

"Whatever for?" asked Sir Harry with a puzzled frown.

"'Tis not so unusual," Olivia pointed out. "Liza had a Season the year before she married George, you know."

"Yes, but your sister had to go to Town to snare a husband. You've no need to go husband-hunting, Livvy, because you've got me," her faithful swain said generously, then hastened to add, "that is, if you'll have me."

"And by this offer, am I to understand that you have seen enough of the world, and are now ready to settle down to the domestic life?" Miss Darby pressed on.

Sir Harry thought wistfully of a certain actress outside whose dressing room he had been wont to camp until his father's untimely demise had recalled him to Leicestershire. Fortunately for the success of his mission, Sir Harry had the wisdom to refrain from making this fair charmer's existence known to his chosen bride. "Much as I enjoy Town life, I know where my duties lie," pronounced Sir Harry loftily. "With Papa gone, I am the head of the family, and now that I am out of mourning, I think it high time I wed. I am sure it would greatly relieve Mama's mind to have me settled."

"Then I suppose I must accept your generous offer," Miss Darby conceded in a voice curiously devoid of emotion. "Far be it from me to disoblige your Mama."

"Capital!" proclaimed Sir Harry, then added in a more serious tone, "It ain't just for Mama's sake, you know. No matter how much she wished it, I wouldn't offer for you if I wasn't certain we should deal famously together."

Miss Darby mustered a smile. "Indeed, I have always thought we would, Harry."

"Of course we will! After all, we've rubbed along tolerably enough for most of our lives. 'Twill be just as before, only different."

With this happy prediction, Sir Harry announced his intention of imparting the good news to his family, and, after bestowing a fraternal kiss on Miss Darby's cheek, took his leave.

His affianced bride remained in the Blue Saloon for several minutes, gazing down at the flowers in her lap—unless she was much mistaken, the same flowers which she had just that morning brought in from the hothouse and arranged in the large urn on the landing. How much had changed in those few hours! Of course, she had known all her life that she would one day marry the heir to the Hawthorne baronetcy, thus fulfilling their fathers' dreams of merging the two estates. Still, there was quite a difference in expecting something to take place in the vague and distant future and seeing it accomplished as fact. Now the betrothal was real. She was to wed Harry, whom she had loved as long as she could remember. And although she entertained no illusions that Harry nursed a grand passion for her, she was well satisfied with her lot. She was certain he would be a kind and considerate husband, when he thought of it, and if he did not love her, at least she had the satisfaction of knowing that she held some small place in his affections, somewhere above that occupied by his hounds, though not so high, perhaps, as his horse. Many ladies, she knew, would envy her.

Yes, she reflected sadly, pressing her gloved hand to her cheek, where Sir Harry's kiss still burned, she was a most fortunate young lady.

While Sir Harry offered his heart and hand to Miss Darby, his sister, a Titian-haired damsel of seventeen, entertained a visitor at Hawthorne Grange. The Reverend James Collier, vicar of Hawthorne parish, was a serious-minded young man of some eight-and-twenty years. He was also remarkably handsome, being possessed of a crop of golden curls, one of which was wont to fall carelessly over the good reverend's aristocratic brow, and a pair of fine blue eyes whose charms were not entirely obscured by wire-rimmed spectacles.

In the six months since this worthy gentleman had assumed the living at Hawthorne, Miss Georgina Hawthorne had experienced a spiritual awakening of no small degree. Once a frivolous damsel who cared for little besides fashions and flirtations, she now devoted herself to the service of the little parish church and its shepherd. Throughout the summer months she had made a practice of providing fresh flowers for the altar every Sabbath, and when winter's icy blasts at last put an end to this activity, she had unwittingly offended the Widow Latham by usurping that good woman's universally acknowledged, albeit unofficial, position as overseer of the altar cloths, bearing them away after each week's service so that they might be laundered and starched by the Grange's own servants and, when necessary, mending them with her own hands. Now, with the vicar taking tea in her parlor, she presented the snowy linens to him, ready to bask in the warmth of his praise. Nor was she disappointed.

"Your devotion, Miss Hawthorne, is an example to us all," said the good reverend, his fingers brushing hers ever so fleetingly as he received the cloths from her hands.

"It was nothing, really," she protested modestly, setting at naught the stain from the Eucharist wine which had taken the under housemaid the better part of an entire morning to eradicate. "'Twas, after all, only my duty as a Christian."

"Would that all my parishioners were as mindful of their duty," he replied with feeling. "Miss Hawthorne, I have often had occasion, over the last six months, to admire the dedication with which you go about your Father's business."

"But my father is dead," protested the literal-minded Miss Hawthorne.

The vicar's handsome face registered mild shock. "I was referring to your *heavenly* Father," he explained with some consternation.

"Oh," said Miss Hawthorne, embarrassed at her *faux pas*. "As to that, Reverend, one does what one can."

"Indeed. And yet, although one may do much good, surely if two were to combine their efforts, they might accomplish twice as much." While his fair hearer digested the mathematics of this statement in silence, the vicar was emboldened to possess himself of her hands. "My dear Miss Hawthorne, will you grant me permission to speak to your brother?"

"Harry?" said Miss Hawthorne with a puzzled frown. "You may speak to him any time you like. Why should I have any objection?"

"Miss Hawthorne, I am asking for your hand in marriage!" said the good reverend, understandably chagrined.

Miss Hawthorne's eyes opened wide. "Oh!" she gasped, taken aback at thus unexpectedly receiving the offer for which she had been angling for the past six months, the achievement of which goal, it must be said, fell short of Miss Hawthorne's rosy imaginings.

"Perhaps I spoke too soon—" hedged the Reverend Mr. Collier, misinterpreting her response.

"Oh, no!" she put in quickly. "I was hoping you would—that is, I should be pleased if you were to speak to Harry. He is out at present, but he should return ere long. And," she confided with a twinkle in her hazel eyes, "you should find him in a receptive mood. He has gone to offer for Olivia."

"Miss Darby?" The vicar nodded his approval. "A most sensible young woman. Perhaps she will be able to restrict that flightiness of character which—" Mr. Collier broke off in confusion. "I beg your pardon, Miss Hawthorne. I should not have spoken so freely of the head of your family."

Miss Hawthorne, however, was not offended. "I don't see why not, for everyone knows it is true," she said with alarming frankness. "But I think she truly cares for him, and so perhaps will be a good influence."

Having settled Sir Harry's future to their mutual satisfaction, the vicar and his chosen bride turned their attentions to their own plans, and remained thus agreeably occupied until Sir Harry returned. He whistled a jaunty tune as he entered the great hall, giving his sister to understand that his mission had been a success.

"Hullo, Georgie," he said, bending over to buss her heartily on the cheek. "It seems you are to have a sister."

"I'm sure I wish you and your bride very happy," put in the vicar.

Unlike the females of the parish, Sir Harry was unmoved by the vicar's charms, and consequently had been unaware of that gentleman's presence until the clergyman spoke. "Good day, Reverend," he said, moving quickly to pump the vicar's hand. "Dashed if you didn't slip up on me! I take it Georgie has already told you the news?"

"Indeed, she has, and I offer you both my heartiest felicitations. Furthermore, since wedding bells seem to be in the air, as it were, I wonder if I might have a word with you in private?"

This preamble, combined with his sister's rosy blush, gave Sir Harry a fair indication of what was in the wind. He had not observed that young lady's newfound religious zeal for the past six months without having a shrewd idea of what she was about, but he had not supposed the vicar to be so obtuse as to be taken in by this pious display.

"Of course, of course!" he said quickly, trying not to betray his surprise. "Right this way. Will you take a drop of brandy? No? Sherry, perhaps?"

Declining all offers of refreshment, the reverend allowed himself to be led into the room which was dubbed Sir Harry's study, although that young man was not by nature studious. Still, the room had served as a study for the previous baronet, and it was to this room that the two men repaired to settle the future of that worthy's daughter. When the door was securely shut behind them, the vicar turned to address his prospective brother-in-law.

"I have often had occasion to admire the many good works which Miss Hawthorne does in the interest of the parish," he said, "and, since the holy scriptures say it is not good for man to be alone, I find my affections have fixed upon her as a suitable help meet. As I have cause to believe Miss Hawthorne is not averse to my suit, I have come to request your permission to pay my addresses."

Knowing Georgina well, Sir Harry was quite certain that she was far from averse to the vicar. Still, the discovery that the Reverend Mr. Collier might entertain similar feelings for his flighty sister was nothing short of mind-boggling.

"Georgie?" he echoed incredulously. "A vicar's wife?"

"I know the living at Hawthorne is not large," confessed the vicar, prepared for objections on financial grounds. "Still, I have some money from my maternal grandmother, and I feel myself to be capable of supporting Miss Hawthorne in a manner which, I believe, you would not despise."

"I don't doubt it, but—dash it, Reverend! She's only seventeen!"

"She is young, it is true, but her devotion to the work of the parish indicates a spiritual maturity beyond her years."

Privately, Sir Harry suspected that his sister's supposed devotion indicated nothing more spiritual than a schoolgirl *tendre* for the vicar, but he kept this observation to himself.

"It ain't just that. She's never even been out of Leicestershire."

"Am I to understand, then, that your scruples have less to do with age than experience?"

"Yes, that's it!  Lack of experience, there's the ticket," said Sir Harry, seizing upon the excuse conveniently provided a scant half-hour earlier by his chosen bride.  Warming to this train of thought, he stroked his sidewhiskers, adding piously, "She needs to see a bit more of the world before becoming leg-shackled—er, entering the bonds of holy matrimony."

"I cannot fault your reasoning, nor your concern for your sister's future happiness," said his would-be relation, nodding his approval. "What, then, do you suggest?"

"Georgie shall go to London to make her come-out," pronounced Sir Harry, improvising rapidly.  "If, by the end of the Season, her feelings are unchanged, the pair of you may marry with my blessing."

The Reverend Mr. Collier, overcome by the wisdom of this Solomonic decree, was moved to shake Sir Harry's hand.  "And, if the frivolities of town life prove too tempting for her to resist, then we shall know she was never cut out for life in the ministry."

"I wish you good fortune, vicar," said Sir Harry, returning the handshake, "but if you were a betting man, I would lay you odds!"

It was not to be expected that Georgina would submit without protest to this test of her devotion; nor did she.

"But I cannot neglect my church work," she objected, upon being informed of the treat in store. "If I go to London, who will see to the altar cloths, or the flowers, or—"

"Cut line, Georgie," said Sir Harry, interrupting this recitation. "The parish church has survived for nigh on three hundred years without you; surely it can bear your absence for three months. And don't tell me you won't enjoy going to balls and the theater, and wearing clothes that are all the crack, for I know you too well."

Georgina gave him a look of pitying disdain. "At one time, perhaps, I might have been tempted by such frivolous pursuits. Fortunately, my dear James has opened my eyes to the futility of a life devoted entirely to pleasure. My feet are now set on a higher path."

"Save it for the reverend," advised her brother with a snort of skepticism. "You'll forget all about your high principles the minute some blade asks you to waltz."

"You may banish me to London, Harry, but you will never prevail upon me to whirl about a public room in the lascivious embrace of any gentleman, be he blade or no."

"No? Not even with your vicar?"

"Oh!" cried an outraged Georgina, her cheeks suffused with an angry flush which, had she but known it, clashed most unfortunately with her coloring. "For your information, James says—"

But Mr. Collier's opinions were destined to remain a mystery, for the quarreling siblings' mother chose that moment to voice her own objections to the proposed scheme.

"My dear Harry, you cannot have thought," she protested in a quavering voice. "I have scarcely put off my blacks! How can I undertake the launching of a lively schoolgirl into society? I am sure my poor nerves would never bear the strain."

Having long acquaintance with his mama's poor nerves, Sir Harry recognized the futility of opposing this argument. "What of Grandmama, then? Perhaps she might be persuaded to take Georgie in hand."

"Your grandmother? Bah!" scoffed his fond parent. "Why, she abandoned London for Bath fifty years ago, and she hasn't set foot outside her lodgings in twenty years—not even for your poor father's funeral, God rest his soul."

"But why should she?" protested Georgina. "You must admit, Mama, there was very little she could have done."

But this argument, however reasonable, found no favor with the widow. "In times of bereavement, one's proper place is with one's Family. There is nothing like the presence of one's nearest and dearest to give one comfort."

"Perhaps she didn't consider us near and dear," pointed out Georgina with youthful candor. "After all, Papa only visited Bath twice a year, and we rarely accompanied him. Indeed, I can scarcely remember Grandmama at all—although I do recall that she bore a most striking resemblance to you, Harry."

"A handsome old girl, in fact" was Sir Harry's irreverent observation.

Actually, the resemblance between Sir Harry and his paternal grandmother was often remarked upon by those who were acquainted with both the dowager and the current baronet. The likeness was generally felt to be a fortuitous one, since the dowager Lady Hawthorne was the daughter of a viscount and bore the physical stamp of her illustrious lineage. To be sure, she would be an impressive patroness for any young girl making her come-out—or she would have been, had she not long since elected to cloister herself in her Laura Place lodgings.

"Failing Grandmama, I've another idea," continued Sir Harry, undaunted. "Olivia is to be brought out this spring; perhaps Mrs. Darby would be willing to take Georgina on, too—with all expenses to be paid by me, of course."

"An excellent notion," nodded his mama in approval, warming to the scheme now that it seemed unlikely to cut up her peace in any way. "You must enlist Miss Darby's aid in bringing her about. Georgina, my dear, you would not object to visiting London in Miss Darby's company, would you, now that you are to be sisters?"

"Not at all, Mama. In fact, James has the greatest admiration for Olivia. He said that he admired her good sense, and that he hoped she would be a settling influence on you, Harry," she added, not without satisfaction.

"I say!" cried that young man, eyes open wide in alarm. "When I settle down, it will be by my own choice, and not through the machinations of some cursed interfering female!"

"That is not at all a proper way to speak of your affianced bride, Harry," scolded his mama.

Thus chastised, Sir Harry had the grace to look ashamed. "You are quite right, Mama, and I beg your pardon. I am a fortunate man to have Olivia for my bride. Besides," he added with a rush of affection for his betrothed, "Livvy ain't the type to begrudge a fellow his pleasures."

# 2

London, thou art the flower of Cities all.
WILLIAM DUNBAR, *London*

For Miss Olivia Darby, the next two months flew by in a blur of preparations for her London debut. The local dressmaker was summoned to take Miss Darby's measurements for the vast wardrobe which, according to her mama, was *de rigueur* for a Season in Town. When she was not submitting to endless fittings, Olivia was enlisted to aid her mother in writing to all that lady's London acquaintances, in the hopes of exploiting these connections to her daughter's advantage. But of her affianced bridegroom Olivia saw little, for Sir Harry, upon learning of Mrs. Darby's intention to hire lodgings in Upper Wimpole Street, objected to seeing his future bride installed at such a *démodée* address, and insisted upon offering Mrs. Darby the use of the Hawthornes' town house in Curzon Street, while he (he said) would content himself with hired rooms more suited to his bachelor status. Upon Mrs. Darby's acceptance of this generous offer, he announced his intention of departing for London within the week to ensure that all was in readiness for their arrival. Mrs. Darby was moved to exclaim at the thoughtfulness of her future son, but Olivia, aware of Sir Harry's fondness for town life, quite correctly ascribed this fit of generosity to more self-serving motives.

Mother and daughter arrived in London in mid-March, along with Sir Harry's sister Georgina, who whiled away the journey by outlining for her companions the various perils of the fashionable life which, according to Mr. Collier, lurked in the Metropolis, ready to devour the unwary. Indeed, any disinterested listener might have supposed their southeasterly course to lead directly to Hell, rather than London. At last they entered the city, its cobbled streets alive with the cries of vendors hawking their wares and the squeals of grubby, unwashed children at play. Upon seeing these unfortunates, Georgina was moved to denounce the *beau monde* for frittering away fortunes on gaming and fashion in the face of such squalor. These noble sentiments, while they would no doubt have found favor with the good reverend, were quite wasted on her intended audience, for the Darbys, both mother and daughter, had long since fallen asleep.

The slumberers at last awoke as the carriage rolled to a stop before the Curzon Street town house, and the ladies exited the vehicle somewhat stiffly. Sir Harry's butler flung open the front door as they mounted the stairs, and the travel-weary trio entered the edifice which was to be their home for the next three months.

"Well," declared Georgina, who had not visited the London house since she was in leading strings and, consequently, feared the mansion might be out of keeping with her newly-acquired democratic notions. "'Tis not nearly so large as I remembered it."

"Nonsense," replied Mrs. Darby, who had no such scruples. "It is a fine house indeed, and it appears dear Harry has done an excellent job of seeing all put to rights."

Only Olivia declined to offer an opinion. Instead, she silently followed her parent into the tiled entrance hall. Here her heart leaped at the sight of a solitary figure which, upon closer inspection, proved to be a very fine piece of statuary set into a niche in the wall.

"Oh," she said, striving in vain to keep her disappointment from showing in her voice. "I thought perhaps Harry would be here."

"But my dear, don't you remember?" prompted her mama. "Harry has taken lodgings in Stratton Street. 'Twould not be at all proper for you to be living under the same roof before you are wed."

"I know, Mama. I only hoped—that is, I thought perhaps he might be here to welcome us."

"I think it very shabby of him not to meet us upon our arrival," concurred Georgina. "Depend upon it, he has probably gone to some dreadful prize-fight or some such thing."

But in this estimation she was mistaken. Sir Harry was, in fact, preparing to visit Covent Garden, where the celebrated actress Violetta was to appear in one of the breeches rôles for which she was so much admired. Enthusiastic patron of the arts that he was, Sir Harry arrived early in order to procure a choice spot in the pit from which he might ogle the fair thespian to his heart's content. It was here that he was hailed by the Honourable Felix Wrexham.

"I say, Harry," remarked this worthy. "Had no idea you was in London. Beginning to think you'd left us for good."

"No, just until my mourning was up. My pater, you know."

"Deuced sorry to hear it, old boy," Mr. Wrexham muttered, ill at ease with the subject of man's mortality. To this gentleman's heartfelt relief, the curtain rose at that moment, revealing the fair Violetta as the heroine of Shakespeare's *Twelfth Night*. For this first act she was clothed in female garb, to the vocal dissatisfaction of her admirers. Fortunately, her rôle as the sole survivor of a shipwreck had given Mr. Kemble the inspired notion of saturating his comedienne's gown with water, so that it clung enticingly to her every curve. It was, perhaps, only this happy circumstance which saved the theater from a mob revolt. By the time the curtain rose on the second act, revealing Violetta in her masculine disguise, her audience was in a much more receptive mood.

"I say, Felix," remarked Harry, elbowing aside a Cit who, overcome with adoration, had pressed forward and consequently blocked Sir Harry's view. "Dashed if she ain't the most delectable morsel I've ever clapped eyes on!"

"No argument from me. Not that we're likely to clap anything else on her," Mr. Wrexham added morosely.

"What do you mean?" asked Sir Harry, his attention momentarily diverted from the stage.

"Islington," was Mr. Wrexham's reply. "She's been under the duke's protection for the last twelvemonth."

Sir Harry's eyebrows rose in surprise. "You don't say! I thought perhaps she favored Mannerly."

"Thought so, myself. If you ask me, there's something dashed havey-cavey about the whole affair. Happened just before you left town, as I recall. Perhaps you remember. Mannerly suddenly took himself off to the Continent, leaving Islington a clear field. Know anything about it?"

Sir Harry turned back to the stage, concealing the telltale flush that stained his cheeks. "No, Felix. Not a thing."

By the time the final curtain fell, Sir Harry had had occasion to recall the arrival of his sister and his future bride. However, a glance at his pocket watch informed him that he would not be thanked for calling on them at this late hour. And so when Mr. Wrexham suggested that they look in at his club, Sir Harry was quick to agree—a profitable enterprise which left him, in the chill gray hours just before dawn, some one hundred guineas to the better. It was only natural that he stayed abed until well into the afternoon to recover from his night of merriment, and so it was that, when the belated bridegroom finally presented himself in Curzon Street, he was met with the information that Mrs. Darby, Miss Darby, and Miss Hawthorne were not at home.

◆

If Miss Darby was disappointed in her lack of a reception, her sentiments were not shared by her mama. In fact, Mrs. Darby congratulated herself on her forethought in writing to all her London acquaintances, for invitations began to arrive in Curzon Street even before she and her charges had taken up residence there. Consequently, their first full day in the Metropolis was filled to overflowing, the morning hours being spent in consultation with Madame Girot, one of London's most fashionable modistes, while the afternoon was devoted to paying calls on the aforementioned acquaintances. Arriving at the town residence of Lady Bainbridge, Mrs. Darby and her charges were greeted with every evidence of enthusiasm by Mrs. Darby's long-ago school friend.

"Elinor Darby, as I live and breathe!" exclaimed her ladyship warmly as the trio was ushered into a modish saloon furnished in airy shades of blue. "How long has it been? And this must be your Olivia," she concluded, grasping Georgina's hands.

"No, no," protested Mrs. Darby. "This is Miss Hawthorne, whose brother is to marry my daughter. *This* is Olivia."

"Why, she is charming!" cried Lady Bainbridge, transferring her effusions to the proper object. "I'm sure I wish you very happy, Miss Darby. But who is the fortunate young man?"

"Sir Harry Hawthorne," replied the beaming bride. Her smile dimmed somewhat as she added, "I regret he could not accompany us today, but—"

"We shall do quite well without him," declared Lady Bainbridge, who had seen to many *ton* marriages to wonder at the prospective bridegroom's absence. "But you must meet my other guests. Elinor, you must remember Lady Sefton and Mrs. Drummond-Burrell; ladies, Mrs. Darby, her daughter Miss Darby, and Miss Hawthorne. Miss Darby is to marry Miss Hawthorne's elder brother, Sir Harry Hawthorne."

Mrs. Darby was in alt. Here under her dear friend's roof were not one, but *two* of Almack's patronesses! Wreathed in smiles, she urged her two charges forward.

"I well remember granting your elder daughter a voucher for Almack's, Mrs. Darby," said Lady Sefton, nodding a greeting. "A lovely girl, as I recall. She married Lord Clairmont, did she not?"

"Yes, and now Liza is in the family way," replied the proud grandmother-to-be. "She hopes to present her husband with an heir by Whitsunday."

"But how unfortunate for all our young men, Miss Darby, to discover that you, too, are already taken!" protested the patroness with a smile, as the new arrivals seated themselves on a sofa of pale blue damask.

Mrs. Drummond-Burrell, generally held to be the starchiest of the seven patronesses in spite of—or perhaps because of—the fact that she was the only one of that select group without a title, remained silent throughout this exchange, but fixed Georgina with a piercing gaze, as if casting about in her mind for a masculine counterpart. "Hawthorne…Hawthorne. I don't believe I am familiar with the name," she declared at last.

Olivia was momentarily surprised by the patroness's disavowal of her beloved, since she had often heard from Sir Harry's own lips of his intimacy with the highest of the *haut ton.* Then she smiled. How very like Harry, and how devastated he would be to know that London's most exclusive sorority did not remember his name!

"Of course you know Sir Harry, Clementina," Lady Sefton prompted, fixing her fellow patroness with a speaking look. "If I mistake not, Miss Darby's fiancé is a particular intimate of Lord Mannerly."

"Ah!" uttered Mrs. Drummond-Burrell cryptically.

"Lord Mannerly?" echoed Olivia. "I have never heard mention of the name."

"You will," predicted Almack's haughtiest patroness sagely. "If you remain in London for any length of time, you will."

"And what of you, Miss Hawthorne?" put in Lady Bainbridge, perhaps a bit too quickly. "Have you any matrimonial ambitions?"

"Indeed, I have," replied that young lady, jutting her chin forward in a manner which could only be described as mulish. "I intend to marry the vicar of our parish, Mr. James Collier."

Lady Sefton shot Mrs. Darby a sympathetic glance. "I see," she said, and Mrs. Darby was left with the impression that she saw a great deal more than Georgina had intended. "Still, I think I had best send you vouchers to Almack's. Perhaps, Miss Hawthorne, you will consent to *waltz* with some of our young men, even if you do not wish to *marry* them."

Georgina could not let this opportunity slip past. "Oh, but I could not! Mr. Collier says—"

"Your ladyship is too kind," interrupted Mrs. Darby, sparing the patronesses the good reverend's most unflattering opinion of the daring German dance. "I am sure my daughter and Miss Hawthorne would be delighted to attend. Indeed, no young lady's Season may be judged a success without it."

Having achieved this *coup*, Mrs. Darby decided not to press her luck. Precisely fifteen minutes after their arrival, she herded her charges into the carriage and set the horses' heads toward Curzon Street, before Georgina could destroy both young ladies' chances with some tactless—though undoubtedly pious—remark. Upon their return, they were greeted with the news that Sir Harry had called and planned to return the following afternoon at five o'clock, at which time he hoped Miss Darby would consent to drive with him in the park. This buoyed that young lady's spirits even more than the projected visit to Almack's, and she retired to her room that night with a much lighter heart.

Alas, the reunion was not an entirely felicitous one. Olivia had dressed with special care in a very fetching carriage gown of rose-colored lutestring, and her appearance was enough to inspire more than one gentleman to inquire as to the identity of the deuced pretty chit riding with young Hawthorne. Unfortunately Sir Harry, absorbed in pointing out the various perfections of his newly-acquired phaeton, was oblivious to the charms of his fair passenger.

In point of fact, Sir Harry was unaccustomed to paying court to ladies of quality, particularly ladies whom he had known since they were in leading strings, and he found himself quite at a loss. So long as he was boasting of his cattle or entertaining his future bride with such *on dits* as might be judged fitting for a lady's ears, he could forget about the betrothal and think of her as the childhood friend with whom he had spent so many carefree days. It was to this less intimidating person, therefore, that he addressed his apologies.

"Deuced sorry I didn't get by to see you last night, Livvy," he said awkwardly, his eyes not quite meeting those of his fiancée. "A previous engagement, you know. I trust you had a pleasant trip?"

"Well enough, although a bit fatiguing. It seems Mr. Collier has much to say about the evils of the Metropolis," she confessed with a mischievous gleam in her eye.

Sir Harry's awkwardness vanished, and he grinned back at her. "In other words, Georgie bored you cock-eyed! Depend upon it, she'll drop her Friday-faced airs the first time she sets foot in Almack's."

"Which may be sooner than you think," replied Olivia with no small satisfaction. "We met Lady Sefton and Mrs. Drummond-Burrell yesterday at Lady Bainbridge's, and they have promised us vouchers."

Sir Harry, well aware of the capriciousness of Almack's patronesses in granting the coveted vouchers, was impressed. "You don't mean it!"

"I do! Although I confess it was a very near thing for a moment, when Georgina started to favor the patronesses with Mr. Collier's views on the waltz."

Sir Harry gave a shout of laughter. "About its being an instrument of the devil? That *would* have set the cat amongst the pigeons, wouldn't it?"

"I shudder to think of it!" replied Olivia, suiting the word to the deed. "But we have vouchers, and Mama says we may attend on Wednesday. Oh, Harry, would you escort us?"

Sir Harry looked askance at the wide blue eyes gazing eagerly up at him. The childhood friend had vanished, and in her place sat the future wife. He ran his finger inside a cravat which suddenly felt too tight.

"Er, I don't know, Livvy," he stammered. "There's a prize fight at Tothill Fields, and I promised Felix—Mr. Wrexham, that is—that I'd go with him. Got a monkey on Molyneux, you know, so I—Hullo, I've got it! I'll meet you there! That's the ticket, Livvy," he said, warming to this product of his own brain. "You go on to Almack's with your mama and Georgie, and I'll meet you there. Only promise to save me the first waltz!"

# 3

Faint heart ne'er won fair lady.
MIGUEL DE CERVANTES, *Don Quixote de la Mancha*

Selwyn St. George, fifth marquess of Mannerly, leaned against the wall at Almack's and studied the dancers with a bored mien. Certainly no one would have guessed by his saturnine countenance that his primary emotion was relief. He flicked open his enameled snuffbox, placed a small pinch of his signature blend on the inside of his wrist, and inhaled deeply. He had been foolish, he now realized, to imagine that one minor mishap with a greenhorn fresh from the wilds of Leicestershire would close Society's doors against one of its most eligible bachelors. If anyone recalled the circumstances surrounding his self-imposed exile from the Metropolis, they gave no outward sign.

But *he* remembered, and the bitter memory caused his black brows to draw together in a frown of such ferocity that one young lady, passing at that moment into his line of vision and supposing herself to be the object of his disapproval, fled to the safety of her mother's arms. He had not spent his entire adult life cultivating an air of jaded sophistication only to have it destroyed in an instant by an impudent young pup still wet behind the ears. Not, he considered, that the pup in question had intentionally emptied his wineglass over the marquess's head; in fact, he doubted the young man possessed that much bottom. No, young—what was his name? Harley? Hawley? Hawthorne? Whoever he was, he was merely trying to catch the eye of the beauteous Violetta, the same as every other male present at Covent Garden on that fateful evening. But far from deriving consolation from this knowledge, Lord Mannerly felt doubly humiliated. It was, after all, more enviable to be the object of a rival's jealousy than merely a hapless victim of circumstance. At any rate, there had been nothing the marquess could do, since to call the young cub out would only have lent him consequence. And so he had quit Covent Garden without further ado, his fashionable Titus crop raining Madeira down his hitherto immaculate shirtfront. He had then made haste to Paris, where he might stroke his wounded *amour propre,* and where shortly thereafter he had heard that the fair Violetta had bestowed her considerable favors upon the Duke of Islington.

"Why, Selwyn, I had no idea you had returned to town," remarked a rather dashing young matron, playfully rapping the marquess's sleeve with her fan. "Have you come to inspect this year's hopefuls? But you do not dance! Shall I help you find a partner?"

"Ever the matchmaker, eh, Emily?" he replied, raising Lady Cowper's gloved hand to his lips with practiced grace. "An exercise in futility, as you surely must know by now. Nevertheless, in order to remain in your good graces, I will do my duty. You may introduce me to—" he paused, raising his quizzing glass to inspect the rainbow of pastel-clad young ladies whirling about the room. At length his sweeping gaze settled on a dark-haired damsel in a gown of purest white shot with silver threads. "—That one." He pointed his glass at the fortunate chosen.

"Miss Darby? She is something out of the common way, is she not? But," added Lady Cowper, dimpling up at him, "I think it only fair to warn you not to entertain any matrimonial hopes where she is concerned. Miss Darby is already betrothed to Sir Harry Hawthorne."

Lord Mannerly's quizzing glass checked ever so briefly before he let it fall. Sir Harry Hawthorne? This, surely, was the intended bride of the young cub who had precipitated his abrupt departure from London. For the first time in many weeks, the marquess's spirits lifted, then soared. How absurd, to think he had spent the better part of a year pouting over a blow to his pride! Selwyn St. George, fifth marquess of Mannerly, sulking over the loss of a bit of muslin who was no better than she should be! His Mannerly forebears must have been setting the family crypt awhirl! But no more. He was a Mannerly, and Mannerlys did not get embarrassed; they got even. As he eyed the dark-haired beauty in white, a plan began to form in his mind—a cunning, clever, brilliant plan. By God, he would teach the impudent young pup to make a fool of the marquess of Mannerly! He would have his revenge, and this nubile nymph was the key. Turning back to Lady Cowper, he flashed his most charming smile.

"Having done your duty by delivering this caveat, my lady," he said, offering her his arm, "lead on!"

"What time is it, Mama?" asked Olivia, fidgeting in the elegant but uncomfortable chair situated along the wall.

"Ten fifty-two," replied her parent placidly, consulting the ormolu clock concealed from her daughter's view by her own plumed turban. "Precisely two minutes later than it was the last time you asked."

"He's not coming, is he?" Olivia asked miserably. "Harry isn't coming."

"Well, if he is, he'd best be quick about it," said Mrs. Darby matter-of-factly. "The doors are locked precisely at eleven, and no one—not even the hero of Waterloo, Wellington himself—is admitted after that hour."

"I suppose I should have known," conceded Olivia with a sigh.

"Indeed, I should think you would, my dear," replied her mama briskly. "After all, why should a young man be expected to dance attendance on his fiancée, with so many other amusements to distract him? Men are all alike, my dear. Predictable, but necessary. They loathe Almack's to a man. But you mustn't take it personally, Olivia. Never mind losing an occasional battle when you have already won the war." Having delivered herself of this sage advice, she bent a frown upon her unhappy daughter. "In my opinion, you were a bit rash in refusing to dance with young Eversley—excellent *ton*, and a sizable fortune, especially for a younger son. Perhaps we might have steered him in Georgina's direction," she added, *sotto voce*, casting a furtive glance at the primrose-clad damsel seated on her other side, who observed the waltz in progress with a marked air of disapproval.

"I thought it only fitting to save my first dance for Harry—indeed, I promised him as much," she confessed. "Unfortunately, it appears that he—"

But Mrs. Darby, eyes widening in anticipation, had lost interest in her daughter's absentee suitor. "Only look, Olivia! Lady Cowper is headed this way, and see the fine gentleman she is bringing with her! If he asks you to dance, my dear, you are to accept. We cannot have you and Georgina labeled as wallflowers."

The next instant saw the Hawthorne party introduced to Lady Cowper's distinguished companion, and although he was scrupulously polite to all three ladies, it was clearly Olivia's presence which had led him thither.

"Lord Mannerly, may I present Mrs. Darby, Miss Darby, and Miss Hawthorne? Lord Mannerly, I believe, is an intimate acquaintance of your fiancé, Miss Darby," added the patroness, darting a mischievous glance at the marquess.

Georgina, seated demurely beside her chaperone, watched as the most striking man she had ever seen bowed over Olivia's hand. She could not in all honesty call him handsome, for his swarthy countenance possessed a magnetism which transcended mere beauty. His hair was the glossy black of a raven's wing, and his dark eyes glittered as if at some private amusement. Georgina was struck with the notion that he would be a dangerous man to cross. She was immediately ashamed of the direction her wayward thoughts had taken. If her brother considered this gentleman a friend, why should she think of him as an enemy?

"I should be honored," Lord Mannerly was saying, "if you would stand up with me for the waltz, Miss Darby."

Olivia, having been warned by her mama not to waltz until being granted permission to do so, glanced at Lady Cowper and, seeing the patroness nodding her approval, took the marquess's proffered hand. "I am sure any friend of Harry's must be a friend of mine," she said as they took their places.

"I have a confession to make," replied Lord Mannerly with a notable lack of repentance. "I fear you were misled. Although I am acquainted with Sir Harry, I cannot in good conscience call any man friend who steals a march on me so unsportingly. Tell me, Miss Darby, how came you to cast your lot with Sir Harry without giving the rest of us poor blighters a chance to win your affections?"

"We are near neighbors, my lord, and it has always been our families' dearest wish that we should wed," explained Olivia.

"Then it is an arranged marriage?"

"Yes—not that we ourselves are reluctant for the match," she added perhaps a bit too quickly.

"My dear Miss Darby, how could any man be reluctant to unite himself to such beauty?" replied Lord Mannerly, guiding her easily through the movements of the dance.

Olivia, having been sadly neglected by her prospective bridegroom, was no match for Lord Mannerly's flowery compliments. Acutely aware of the admiration in his black eyes and the warm pressure of his hand upon her waist, she responded to his flattery much as a flower responds to the sun. Mannerly, observing her shining eyes and heightened color, found himself rearranging his plans. His first thought was to court Miss Darby until she gave young Hawthorne the mitten, thus avenging his own humiliation by seeing his foe publicly jilted. But now, seeing the rise and fall of her white bosom above the *décolletage* of her gown, he revised his plans along more effective—and far more pleasant—lines. He would seduce the love-starved Miss Darby and, since the soiled bride would then undoubtedly hurry her cuckolded swain to the altar as quickly as possible, he would have his revenge on the happy couple's wedding night, when Sir Harry Hawthorne discovered too late that he had been beaten, as it were, to the post. Lord Mannerly's one regret was that his very public humiliation must be satisfied with a very private revenge; but that, he supposed, was the price of genius.

☙

The prospective bridegroom, entering Almack's precisely at ten fifty-seven, paused for a moment inside those hallowed portals, raising his quizzing glass to search for his chosen bride. There was her mama, seated beside Georgie along the wall. Lord Mannerly, he observed with a grimace, was back in Town, and had naturally staked his claim on the most beautiful woman present, a dark-haired enchantress in white. The quizzing glass lingered on this vision briefly before passing on, then returned with a jerk. Livvy! *His* Livvy, in a diaphanous cloud of white sarcenet with a low-cut *corsage* that exposed far too much rounded bosom for his peace of mind. And Lord Mannerly, he observed with displeasure, was taking full advantage of the view. A long-dormant demon of jealousy stirred in Sir Harry's hitherto complacent breast. Mannerly had no business looking at Livvy that way! Dash it all, *he* had no business looking at her that way, and he was all but married to the girl!

As the violins scraped to a halt, Sir Harry charted a direct course for his future mama-in-law, and reached that good lady just as Lord Mannerly returned his fair partner to her mother's side.

"Why, Harry!" exclaimed Olivia, still flushed and breathless from the exertions of the dance. "I had quite given you up."

"So I see," he remarked, glaring at the marquess. "But it appears you have not lacked for partners in my absence. Shall we?" Without waiting for a reply, he seized her gloved hand and all but dragged her back onto the floor, acknowledging Lord Mannerly's presence with naught but a curt nod.

Olivia's first thought upon seeing her betrothed was how splendid he looked in form-fitting knee-breeches and a dark cutaway coat over a watered silk waistcoat, his sandy locks brushed into the fashionable Brutus style. His odd behavior, however, quickly drove sartorial concerns from her mind.

"Why, Harry!" she exclaimed, following him onto the floor. "Whatever is the matter?"

"I might well ask you the same question! Do you have any idea with whom you were dancing?"

"Only your friend, Lord Mannerly," she replied, all at sea.

As the movement of the dance brought them near to the wall, Sir Harry swept his partner out of the mass of dancers and through a brocade curtain into a secluded alcove.

"You have been misinformed," he said bluntly, safe within the privacy of this antechamber. "Mannerly is no friend of mine, and he is not at all a proper person for you to know."

Olivia's blue eyes opened wide with surprise. "But I thought him charming!"

"Oh, he is charming, I'll grant you that," said Sir Harry darkly. "Nevertheless, you will oblige me by having nothing more to do with him."

The meek Miss Darby who had arrived in London the previous week would have denied him nothing; however, the casual neglect of one gentleman, contrasted with the frank admiration of another, had taken its predictable toll. Olivia drew herself up to her full height, her chin thrust obstinately forward.

"You forget yourself, Harry," she replied with remarkable composure. "I have taken no vows to honor and obey you yet, and until that day, I will choose my friends to please myself. If you object to my dancing with Lord Mannerly, I must point out that, if you had torn yourself away from your prize fight earlier, you might have circumvented that undesirable occurrence by the simple expedient of dancing with me yourself."

"Dash it all, Livvy, I'll not—"

But before Sir Harry could voice his objections, the heavy brocade curtain was swept aside, and none other than Lord Mannerly himself raised his quizzing glass to examine the betrothed couple.

"I beg pardon," he drawled lazily. "I seem to have interrupted a lovers' *tête-à-tête.*"

"What do you want, Mannerly?" growled Sir Harry.

"Why, only to ask Miss Darby for the pleasure of another dance," he replied, sweeping a bow in her direction.

Olivia threw a darkling glance at her bridegroom, then bestowed a brilliant smile on the marquess. "I should like it of all things, my lord."

"A charming young lady, Hawthorne," said Mannerly, taking Olivia's hand and drawing it through his arm. "I congratulate you on having won such a prize!"

And, bearing away said prize, he exited the small chamber, leaving Sir Harry to grind his teeth in impotent rage.

He knew, too late, that he had handled it badly, but he could think of no way to explain his dislike of Lord Mannerly without involving Violetta of Covent Garden fame. Further complicating matters was the shock of discovering that Livvy had turned into a diamond of the first water. Equally surprising was her unprecedented display of temper; he had always found her so gentle and eager to please. Without knowing exactly why, he had the sudden and certain feeling that tonight's ill-advised display of jealousy was one he would soon live to regret. Certainly she would never listen to him now, at least not where Mannerly was concerned. Perhaps if another woman were to warn her of the marquess's reputation as a rakehell, were to keep a watchful eye on her, she might pay heed. But Mrs. Darby was unlikely to take his part against her own daughter, and Georgie still needed a keeper herself. If only his mother were out of mourning, or his grandmother were not cloistered in Bath!

At the thought of his grandmother, Sir Harry's expression grew pensive. He had laid eyes on his paternal grandmother exactly twice in his life: once when he was ten years old, and again last spring, when he had made the journey to Bath shortly after his father's death. His impression on the first meeting had been of a fierce dragon of a woman; on the second, a black-draped crow. However, a more impartial miniature in the gallery at Hawthorne Grange, painted some half a century earlier, revealed a feminine version of himself, with a mass of sandy hair, a pair of hazel eyes, and a square, determined jaw.

His thoughts flew back to Covent Garden and the beauteous Violetta, playing Shakespeare's heroine in doublet and hose. He stroked his chin thoughtfully as a plan began to form in his brain. If a woman could disguise herself as a man, he reasoned, why should not a man disguise himself as a woman?

This idea, having taken up residence in his brain, refused to be dislodged. He exchanged social pleasantries with Mrs. Darby, stood up for a country dance with his sister and a very chilly cotillion with Olivia, but all the while his mind was working feverishly. By the time he escorted his ladies home and returned to his rooms in Stratton Street, he was ready to put his plan into action.

"Good evening, sir," said his valet, Higgins, coming forward to remove his master's coat. "I trust you had a pleasant evening?"

"Very," replied Sir Harry, although his tight lips and flashing eyes gave the lie to this statement. He allowed his man to divest him of coat, waistcoat, and cravat, then began to issue the instructions that would put his plan in motion. "Upon the morrow, Higgins, I shall require you to carry out a few errands. I need a wardrobe suitable for a lady of, say, seventy years."

Over a long and varied career, Higgins had occasionally been enlisted to aid one or another of his employers in the pursuit of some lightskirt, but in his admittedly limited experience, these fashionable impures were usually much younger.

"I—I beg your pardon, sir?" Higgins asked, not at all certain he had heard his young master correctly.

"Yes, I should say the old girl is at least seventy. Something in lavender, I suppose, and cut high at the neck, if you will."

"Yes, sir," nodded a dazed Higgins. "And according to what measurements?"

"My own, you nodcock! Who else would I be purchasing clothing for? Furthermore, I shall need undergarments, and—" Heedless of his stunned servant, Sir Harry made a vague gesture in the direction of his chest. "—Something to fill 'em up with. Also a wig, one of those powdered things like old Lady Letton wears. I've no idea where one buys them, but I'm sure they must be available somewhere. You shall make inquiries."

"Yes, sir," replied Higgins in faltering tones.

"But be discreet, mind you!"

"I shouldn't dream of being otherwise," vowed his servant, reflecting that the young master had gone round the bend, just like the poor old King. "Will there be anything else, sir?"

"Just one more thing." Turning toward the looking glass, Sir Harry studied his reflection for a long moment until his image faded and disappeared, replaced with the less pleasant picture of Olivia waltzing by in the marquess of Mannerly's arms. Stroking his sidewhiskers almost lovingly, he commanded, "Shave 'em off, Higgins."

# 4

What strange creatures brothers are!
JANE AUSTEN, *Mansfield Park*

In the sunny parlor of her family's elegant town house, Miss Georgina Hawthorne fairly twitched with impatience, while gentlemen of every description gravitated toward her future sister-in-law like moths to a flame. Although she was genuinely fond of Olivia, Georgina could not quite suppress the unchristian feelings of jealousy that gnawed at her heart. This, she discovered, was how virtue was to be rewarded! It seemed that one who stood up for one's principles was doomed to sit neglected in a corner, while masculine admiration was heaped upon those who had stood up merely for the waltz! Georgina, who had only recently been hailed as the belle of Leicestershire, was unused to such treatment. It had not been easy for her to sit demurely at Mrs. Darby's side, rejecting all efforts to tempt her onto the dance floor. Perhaps worst of all was the knowledge that

Mr. Collier was far away in Leicestershire, unaware of her sacrifice. If only he were there to tell her how much he admired her strength of character, to press her hand, perhaps even to kiss her fingers . . . .

A roar of laughter seemed to mock her wayward thoughts, and she darted an envious glance toward the little group clustered around the sofa where Olivia sat beside the marquess of Mannerly. The gentlemen were heartily amused by something Lord Mannerly had said, while Olivia's pleasure in the marquess's company was betrayed by the roses blooming in her cheeks.

Mrs. Darby, fond parent though she was, tore her eyes away from this evidence of her daughter's success long enough to pat the hand of her young charge. "I told you so," Mrs. Darby reminded Georgina sympathetically, quite correctly interpreting that damsel's silence. "Gentlemen tend to be put off by a young lady with too much virtue."

"No doubt they would prefer a lady with too little," Georgina muttered, but as Mrs. Darby would no doubt have taken this envious outburst as an aspersion on her daughter's character, it was perhaps fortunate that she was distracted by the appearance of the butler announcing a new arrival.

"The Dowager Lady Hawthorne," Coombes announced woodenly, stepping aside to make way for a tall, solidly built matron to enter.

Georgina promptly forgot her troubles, her eyes widening at the unexpected reappearance of her grandmother. She had not seen her paternal grandmother since she was a child, but the old lady's elaborately curled and powdered coiffure was exactly as she remembered it; indeed, Georgina doubted if her grandmother's style of hair dressing had changed in twenty years. A closer inspection, however, revealed that time had indeed left its mark on the elder Lady Hawthorne. The dowager leaned heavily upon an ebony cane, although Georgina was quite certain that at the time of her visit, the old lady's steps had been quick and sure. Her eyes, however, were still bright, and her square-jawed face was remarkably free of wrinkles—a circumstance which caused Georgina's eyes to narrow in suspicion. But of her private misgivings Georgina said nothing, merely rising to greet her aged relation.

"Grandmama! What a pleasant surprise," she said aloud, crossing the room to press her dewy cheek to the old lady's powdered one. "Harry!" she hissed in an undervoice. "Have you run quite mad?"

"I think I must have, for I feel dashed silly," replied her relative in like manner. "And how you females manage to walk in these deuced uncomfortable shoes is a mystery to me."

"But what are you doing here, and in that get-up?"

"I have come to meet my grandson's bride," he announced in a high falsetto. "And if you are referring to my lavender merino, young lady, I beg leave to inform you that this gown happens to be all the crack for ladies who are past the first blushes of youth."

"I—I am sure it is," replied Georgina, demurely lowering her gaze in order to conceal her laughter. "Come with me, ma'am, and I shall introduce you to Miss Darby." Seizing the square hand straining the seams of a white kid glove, Georgina led her relative to the sofa where Olivia sat laughing at Lord Mannerly's latest sally. "Grandmama, may I present Miss Darby, Harry's fiancée? Miss Darby, my—my grandmother, the dowager Lady Hawthorne."

Georgina enlarged upon the introduction to include the bevy of gentlemen who comprised Olivia's court of admirers, but Harry, taking Olivia's gloved hand, heard nothing but the pounding of his own heart. His sister, it seemed, had recognized him instantly; would his fiancée penetrate his disguise as easily? If she betrayed him before Mannerly, well, there would be nothing for it but to sail for America, or perhaps India. Certainly he could not remain on British soil; his humiliation would be too great. For the first time, he wondered what had possessed him to adopt this crack-brained scheme. He strongly suspected Almack's Assembly Rooms of serving something stronger than the lukewarm lemonade for which they were notorious.

For her part, Olivia stared mesmerized at the specimen which would soon be her relative by marriage. She had known that Harry was said to resemble his grandmother; she, too, had seen the Romney portrait at Hawthorne Grange, but nothing had prepared her for the vision which stood before her. The warm hazel eyes, the breadth of shoulder, the square jaw and the large, mannish hand clasping hers—if she did not know better she could almost suppose. . . . But of course poor Lady Hawthorne could not help her mannish appearance. It was unkind to indulge in such foolish imaginings at an old lady's expense.

"How do you do, my lady?" she murmured, moving over to make room on the sofa for the dowager.

"So you're the chit Harry plans to marry," said the old lady in shrill accents. With a contemptuous glance at Olivia's circle of admirers, he added, "My grandson is a fine young man. Make you an excellent husband!"

"I'm sure he will, ma'am," agreed Miss Darby dutifully.

"So tell me, child, what d'ye think of London?"

"Oh, I like it of all things!" Olivia said brightly, unwilling to confess before witnesses that Sir Harry's infrequent appearances made her Season something less than brilliant. "We visited Almack's last night, and tonight Lord Mannerly has offered to escort us to Covent Garden. Is that not generous of him?" she added, with a smile for the marquess.

"Generous, indeed," concurred the dowager with a nod, fixing Mannerly with a purposeful eye. "I daresay I have not set foot in a theater in a quarter of a century. Much has changed since then, I'll warrant."

Lord Mannerly saw the look in that eye, and conceived a dislike for the septuagenarian almost as profound as that which he harbored toward her interfering grandson. He had the greatest aversion to being trapped by any female, be she seventeen or seventy. But as it could hardly further his cause with Miss Darby to deliver a stinging set-down to the grandmother of her fiancé, he merely bared his teeth in a smile noticeably devoid of humor. "I should be honored, Lady Hawthorne, if you would join my party."

"The honor will be all mine, I am sure," replied Sir Harry with unholy glee, having a fair idea of the emotions warring behind the marquess's urbane façade. "You may call for me here, if you please, at eight o'clock. And do be prompt—I abhor dawdlers." Bracing himself with his ebony cane, Sir Harry hoisted himself off the sofa and onto his aching feet. "And now, if I am to enjoy such a treat tonight, I must return to my lodgings and rest. Georgina, dear child, you may see me to my carriage."

"Yes, Grandmama," said that young lady, eagerly seizing the opportunity for a moment alone with her brother. She grabbed the old lady's arm and propelled her out of the parlor at a speed quite unsuited for the dowager's advanced years. Having reached the black-and-white tiled entry hall, however, she turned on her sibling. "All right, Harry, now will you tell me the reason for this ridiculous charade?"

"Shhh!" hissed Sir Harry, darting a furtive glance toward the parlor door. "It's that Mannerly fellow. I don't like him, Georgie."

A tingle of excitement chased down Georgina's spine. So her instincts regarding Lord Mannerly had not been so far off the mark! "Why not?" she asked, agog with curiosity. "What has he done?"

"The tale is not fit for a lady's ears," replied Sir Harry piously. "Suffice it to say that Mannerly detests me as much as I dislike him, and would not hesitate to serve me an ill turn if he had the chance."

The violence of her own reaction to the marquess's blatant masculinity was enough to convince Georgina that her brother might indeed have reason to be concerned. "*That* I can readily imagine! But why the disguise?"

"Because he's a loose fish, Georgie, and I'll not have him sniffing around Livvy in that curst encroaching way of his. As a lady of, er, mature years, I shall be able to keep an eye on Livvy without her being the wiser."

Miss Hawthorne regarded her brother with a knowing eye. "You forbade Olivia to have anything to do with him, didn't you, Harry?" It was a statement, not a question.

"Dashed right, I did!"

"I thought as much. Really, Harry, how could you be so foolish? Surely you must have known you would drive her straight into his arms!"

"No, I didn't! Indeed, why should I?" Sir Harry demanded, justifiably outraged. "I thought she was a sensible girl who would listen to the advice of her future husband!"

Georgina, unimpressed with this speech, rolled her eyes heavenward. "Men! Or women," she amended quickly, casting a dubious glance at her brother's female garb. "Whatever you are, Harry, I vow I'll never understand you!"

ᘓ

With his sister's parting shot still ringing in his ears, Sir Harry returned to Stratton Street and laid aside his disguise. Half an hour saw him back in Curzon Street, this time in his own persona. He tossed his hat and gloves to an unsuspecting Coombes, then mounted the stairs to the parlor, where Mrs. Darby was still receiving callers. Lord Mannerly, he noted with satisfaction, was no longer among their number.

"Why, Harry!" cried Mrs. Darby, holding out her hands to her future son-in-law. "You will never credit it, but your grandmama has returned to Town! If you had arrived a little earlier, you might have seen her yourself, for she paid us a visit not an hour ago!"

Sir Harry expressed his surprise at this unexpected pleasure, then greeted his sister with a smile of bland innocence before turning his attention to his primary object. Here his resolution wavered as he remembered their heated words at Almack's. Should he play the wronged lover, or the apologetic suitor? He wrestled briefly with indecision before rejecting both rôles in favor of cautious formality.

"Your servant, Livvy," he said, raising her hand to his lips. "I trust I find you well?"

Olivia responded in kind. "Quite well, Harry, and—why, Harry! You have shaved your sidewhiskers!" she exclaimed, every trace of constraint banished.

"Well, yes," admitted Sir Harry, rubbing his newly shorn jaw self-consciously. He was unused to the sight of himself *sans barbe*, and the face that had stared back at him from his looking-glass that morning following Higgins's operation had seemed strangely unfamiliar. "I daresay they would have soon been *passé* anyway, now that Brummell has shaven his."

Privately, Olivia felt their removal an improvement, although Sir Harry would have been less than pleased to learn that his clean-shaven look reminded her forcibly of the boy she had once followed about on her pony, in those halcyon days before he had discovered a preference for Town life. These fond reflections she kept to herself, turning her attention back to her mama, who was engaged in making Sir Harry known to the other callers. Foremost among these was a stout matron and her pretty daughter, a petite blonde in a demure sprig muslin gown who nevertheless assessed the new arrival with a predatory eye.

"Mrs. Brandemere, Miss Brandemere, may I present my future son-in-law, Sir Harry Hawthorne? Mrs. Brandemere and her daughter are in London for Miss Brandemere's come-out," explained Mrs. Darby as Sir

Harry made his bow.

"*Sir* Harry Hawthorne, is it?" asked the matron, training an appraising stare upon the newcomer. "Knight, or baronet?"

"Baronet," replied Sir Harry.

Mrs. Brandemere nodded. "I thought you looked a bit young to have already been knighted, although it seems all one must do these days is loan Prinny a large enough sum of money. Better to be a baronet, at any rate, since your son will be a 'sir' someday. 'Tis a great pity you are not a 'lord,' but I daresay you will do very well for Miss Darby."

"Mama, pray don't start that again," begged Miss Sylvia Brandemere, although her fluttering eyelashes and simpering smile belied her protestations.

"You must know, Sir Harry, that I have every expectation of someday hearing my daughter addressed as 'your ladyship,' if not 'your Grace.' Although such an advantageous match for the daughter must be a disadvantage to the mother—imagine how very odd I shall feel when she precedes me in to dinner!"

"Now, Mama, I am sure Sir Harry does not care who I should marry!" protested the future peeress, giving Sir Harry a look which clearly invited him to contradict this statement.

Much to his relief, he was spared the necessity of framing a reply by the gallant intervention of the parlor's only other male occupant, a white-haired gentleman of imposing size whose creaking movements betrayed the necessity of a Cumberland corset to restrain his girth.

"On the contrary, Miss Brandemere, on that day every young man in England will mourn. Why, if I were fifty years younger, I would wish for a coronet myself, so that I might lay it at your feet."

The widowed Mrs. Brandemere, who was not averse to making a second marriage herself, fairly beamed with pleasure. "Oh, prettily said, Colonel! I am sure you would make any woman a worthy suitor, title or no!"

The colonel gave a soulful sigh. "That might have been true at one time, Mrs. Brandemere, but alas, my heart was long since lost to this young man's grandmother. You are the dowager Lady Hawthorne's grandson, are you not?" asked the colonel, addressing himself to Sir Harry.

"I am indeed, sir."

"I knew her when she was still the Honourable Harriet Langford. Fine figure of a woman, your grandmama! I regret that I, too, arrived too late to see her. You've a great look of her about you, if I may say so."

"So I have often been told," acknowledged Sir Harry with a smile.

"Lady Hawthorne accompanies us to Covent Garden tonight," Olivia told him. "May we hope to see you there?"

Sir Harry's smile faded. "No, er, that is, I should have liked to, of course, but a previous engagement—can't be broken at this late date—you understand—"

"Of course. I should not dream of inconveniencing you," replied Olivia stiffly, never suspecting that Sir Harry was likely to find the night's entertainment very inconvenient indeed.

# 5

These troublesome disguises which we wear.
JOHN MILTON, *Paradise Lost*

As her maid applied the finishing touches to her coiffure, Olivia looked forward to the evening's *divertissement* with a variety of conflicting emotions. To be sure, she would have been less than female had she not enjoyed being the object of so much admiration from no less a personage than the marquess of Mannerly; and yet her pleasure in her own success was considerably lessened by the fact that Sir Harry, while quick to warn her away from the marquess, was not sufficiently disturbed by the connection to squire her about London himself. From *on dits* he had let fall in Leicestershire, she had the impression that Sir Harry frequented Covent Garden quite often while in Town. Perhaps, she thought wistfully, it had been in the hopes of seeing him there that she had accepted Lord Mannerly's invitation so eagerly. How, she wondered, might Harry react when he discovered that she had deliberately defied him, and had accepted the marquess's escort? A little shiver of anticipation coursed through her as she imagined Sir Harry in a jealous rage, declaring his undying love for her.

Alas, a light tap on her door banished this thrilling image.

"Olivia?" Mrs. Darby's voice permeated the heavy wooden paneling. "Are you ready, my dear? Lady Hawthorne is here, and Lord Mannerly should arrive at any minute."

"Coming, Mama." Turning to her pier glass, Miss Darby paused to study her reflection critically. It was, of course, impossible to judge one's own appearance objectively, but Olivia thought she looked well enough in a cleverly designed evening gown with a low-cut bodice of black velvet over a skirt of filmy white crêpe. Was it too much to hope, she wondered wistfully as she pulled on her long white kid gloves, that Harry might think her pretty? She made a moue at her image and turned away. Whatever the shortcomings in her appearance, staring into her looking glass was unlikely to alter them.

She allowed her maid to drape her velvet evening cloak over her shoulders, then followed her mother down the curved staircase. There was Lady Hawthorne, resplendent in plum-colored velvet cut high to the throat in direct contradiction to the current fashion for décolletage. Her powdered locks were dressed with purple ostrich plumes which, combined with the lady's already impressive height, were guaranteed to block the view of anyone unfortunate enough to be seated behind her.

"Lady Hawthorne," said Olivia, making her curtsy to this vision. "You look quite splendid. I trust you rested well this afternoon?"

"Quite well, thank you. Come and give me a kiss, my child."

Obediently, Olivia touched her lips to the dowager's cheek. The dutiful peck acted upon her with all the force of an electric shock. A strange sensation, entirely new and yet somehow familiar, washed over her, leaving her unnerved and shaken. Olivia would have searched Lady Hawthorne's face for any sign that the older woman was aware of the current which had seemed to pass between them, but at that moment Lord Mannerly was announced, and the moment was lost.

Olivia hastily composed herself as the marquess made his bow to Georgina, who was looking exceptionally fine in a gown of willow green satin. Upon seeing Olivia, Lord Mannerly lost interest in the flame-haired charmer and crossed the hall to seize Olivia's hands in a warm grasp.

"Ah, Miss Darby! You are in such glowing looks tonight that I can only suppose your betrothed intends to honor us with his presence."

"Not tonight, I'm afraid," Olivia replied, hoping her disappointment could not be heard in her voice. "He has already made plans."

"My grandson has no great love for the stage," put in the dowager firmly.

Lord Mannerly's black brows rose in mild surprise. "Has he not? But I have seen him at Covent Garden on numerous occasions. Or can it be that Sir Harry is not a lover of drama, but of the fair Violetta?"

"Who is Violetta?" asked Olivia, all at sea.

"An actress, Miss Darby. She is generally held to be a great beauty, and her comedic talent often draws comparisons to Mrs. Jordan in her younger days."

"Oh," said Olivia, wishing she had not asked.

"And now, since we are all here," said Lord Mannerly, noting with satisfaction that Miss Darby had lost some of her sparkle, "may I suggest we go? I should prefer to arrive ahead of the crush."

Finding the ladies in agreement, Lord Mannerly bid farewell to Mrs. Darby, promising to return her charges before the hour was too far advanced, then turned to offer his arm to Lady Hawthorne, the highest ranking lady among his guests. This scene almost proved too much for Georgina, who was hard pressed to stifle a giggle at the sight of her brother accepting the escort of the dashing marquess. What, she wondered, would be Lord Mannerly's reaction if he discovered that the lady on his arm was no lady at all, but a man—a man whom, if her brother were to be believed, the marquess hated? Lord Mannerly did not strike her as a gentleman with a lively sense of humor. He would no doubt be livid at being made a laughingstock. Georgina could well imagine the marquess in a towering rage, and in the end, it was nothing less than her fear of Sir Harry's exposure and subsequent humiliation which compelled Miss Hawthorne to keep her countenance.

Once outside, Lord Mannerly handed the person he believed to be the dowager Lady Hawthorne into the elegant crested carriage waiting beside the curb. Sir Harry, in the meantime, had discovered there were certain advantages to his masquerade, as when he had demanded—and received—a kiss of Miss Darby. Quick to press his advantage, he took his place on the upholstered seat and, when Olivia was handed up behind him, reached out to take her hand.

"Come and sit beside me, my dear," he urged, patting the seat beside him.

Since Miss Darby was too well-bred to deny this request, Sir Harry was rewarded with her company for the length of the drive, while Lord Mannerly had to content himself with Georgina in the seat opposite.

Upon reaching the theater, Lord Mannerly ushered his ladies inside, where they retired to the ladies' cloak room to divest themselves of their outer garments. Sir Harry, his disguise affording him unprecedented access to this *sanctum sanctorum*, was not unnaturally mesmerized by the sight of so much feminine beauty primping and preening before the full-length mirrors, until he turned and beheld his fiancée in all her black-and-white splendor.

"I say—that is, my dear Miss Darby, surely you do not intend to go out in public dressed like that!"

All Olivia's earlier doubts about her attire came flooding back. "'Tis the black bodice, is it not?" she said, frowning at her reflection.

"Does it make me look as if I were in mourning?"

"I never saw anyone look less funereal," the dowager informed her roundly. "Why, the neckline is cut so low it's positively indecent!"

Since Olivia's décolletage was in fact quite respectable, she felt compelled to point out the injustice of this charge. "But my lady, this dress is quite modest, compared to some."

Looking about him at the expanse of white flesh on display, Sir Harry was forced to concede the point. "Well, don't come crying to me when you catch your death of cold," muttered her indignant ladyship.

Olivia's ordeal, however, was far from over. When she rejoined Lord Mannerly in the lobby, he bent upon her a look filled with consternation.

"My dear Miss Darby, surely you do not intend to wear that gown to the theater!" he murmured in an undervoice.

"Is it truly so dreadful?" asked Olivia, filled with remorse. "I did wonder about the black bodice, but Madame Girot said—"

"Clearly this Madame Girot is no patron of the arts," replied the marquess, dismissing the unfortunate modiste with a careless wave of his white-gloved hand. "How else could she expect me to follow the play with such an Incomparable seated beside me?"

Relief flooded Miss Darby's countenance, and beneath the much-maligned black velvet bodice, her heart beat faster. "Fie on you, my lord," she scolded playfully. "And how can *I* watch the play, with you turning my head so shamelessly?"

"Harrumph!"

Olivia turned to find a disapproving Lady Hawthorne emerging from the cloak room, followed by a wide-eyed Georgina.

"Oh, I beg your pardon, Lady Hawthorne. I should have waited for you."

"No doubt you were busy," replied the old lady, glowering at Lord Mannerly.

As the quartet took their places in Lord Mannerly's box, Sir Harry discovered there was a price to be paid for his earlier *coup* in procuring a seat beside Olivia, for Lord Mannerly, having thus been forewarned, was forearmed against this maneuver. He was careful to seat grandmother and granddaughter together in the front of his box, leaving himself to sit beside Miss Darby in the rear. Sir Harry, who was well aware of the shadows cloaking the back of the box, and who, over the course of his checkered London career, had had more than one opportunity to steal a kiss under the cover thereof, was understandably less than pleased with this turn of events.

"Surely you cannot wish to sit in the back, my dear," he protested in his best falsetto. "Exchange places with me, Miss Darby, so that you may have a better view of the stage."

"No, no, this is quite all right," insisted Olivia, although the ostrich plumes adorning Sir Harry's powdered wig did in fact obscure much of the stage. "I remember your remarking on how long it has been since you have been to the theater, my lady, and I could not bring myself to deprive you of your excellent vantage point."

Having used this very excuse to procure an invitation to join the party, Sir Harry could hardly inform his betrothed that he had visited Covent Garden less than a se'ennight earlier, and had already seen the company's production of *Twelfth Night*. Thus hoist on his own petard, he had no choice but to accept the seating arrangements without further protest.

At last the curtain rose on the first act, revealing the famed comedienne Violetta as an unlikely shipwreck victim, her sodden garments clinging to her every curve while her ebony curls remained miraculously dry.

"Oh, how lovely she is!" Olivia remarked enviously, leaning nearer the marquess in order to see past Sir Harry's plumes.

"Do you find her so?" asked Lord Mannerly. "She is accounted a great beauty, but I confess in my present company, I find the fair Violetta's charm quite escapes me."

Whatever Olivia might have said to this piece of flattery was drowned out by a fit of coughing from the front of the box. Mannerly was right, damn his eyes, thought Sir Harry. Compared to his Livvy, Violetta's beauty seemed overblown, as if she were trying a bit too hard to enchant. Finding nothing on the stage to interest him, he had no alternative but to listen to Lord Mannerly pay flowery compliments to his fiancée. When at last the curtain fell signaling the interim, Sir Harry judged it high time to put an end to the provoking *téte-â-téte*.

"Miss Darby, my dear, my poor old bones feel quite stiff," he said, lending authenticity to the claim by rising unsteadily to his feet. "Will you give me your arm for a turn about the lobby?"

Olivia obediently rose and offered the dowager her escort. As the pair moved toward the curtained entrance to the box, Lord Mannerly followed Miss Darby's progress appreciatively. It was, he considered, one of the happier consequences of the current fashion for narrow skirts that the gentle sway of a lady's hips was evident as she walked—a sight which had been concealed by fuller skirts twenty years earlier when, as a lad of sixteen, he had first discovered the gentler sex. Shifting his gaze slightly, he noticed that the alluring motion was curiously absent from Lady Hawthorne's shuffling gait. Curious, too, that while the old lady and her grandson were so much alike in other ways, Lady Hawthorne was a tall woman, while Sir Harry's height was not much above the average. In fact, Mannerly supposed them to be very nearly of a height, perhaps about five feet nine inches.

"An interesting woman, your grandmother," he remarked idly to Georgina. "She seems quite attached to Miss Darby."

"Yes, I believe he—that is, Grandmama is very fond of Olivia," improvised that young lady, although her grandmother and Miss Darby had in fact never met. Only Georgina's hands, nervously twisting the strings of her reticule around one gloved finger, betrayed her agitation at finding herself alone with her brother's adversary. "The engagement is one of long standing, you know."

Lord Mannerly nodded. "Miss Darby once intimated as much." He judged it time to turn the subject, but had little experience in—or indeed, desire for—conversing with schoolgirls. "And what of you, Miss Hawthorne? Have you any long-standing arrangements of your own?"

"Yes—well, the attachment is not long-standing, but I am to marry Mr. James Collier, the vicar of our parish."

The marquess's only response was a snort of derisive laughter.

Georgina's eyes narrowed. "You find this amusing, my lord?"

"Vastly. Never have I met anyone who looked less suited to a living in the Church. The flames of hell, my dear, could burn no brighter than your fiery locks."

Up came Miss Hawthorne's chin, all nervousness replaced by outrage. "And never have *I* received such an unhandsome compliment!"

"You must acquit me, Miss Hawthorne. I assure you, I never pay compliments. I speak only the truth as I see it."

Georgina gave a disdainful sniff. "I see. Then I suppose the praise you see fit to lavish on Miss Darby is something in the way of a scientific observation."

"Jealous, Miss Hawthorne?" asked Lord Mannerly with a mocking smile. "For shame! What would your vicar say?"

"I am *not* jealous, and I have no desire for your admiration!" cried Georgina hotly. "You might not credit it, my lord, but there are some gentlemen who consider beauty of the spirit more important than a pretty face and a pleasing figure."

"I am sure your principles do you credit, Miss Hawthorne, but I wonder, if you had been hunch-backed or hare-lipped, would your reverend have been so eager to take you to wife?"

An angry crimson flooded Georgina's face, but good breeding compelled her to bite back the stinging retort which, she was forced to admit, would probably have accomplished nothing but win one of Mannerly's odiously mocking smiles.

While Georgina crossed swords with the marquess, Olivia and "Lady Hawthorne" joined the crowd milling about the lobby, nodding and bowing to acquaintances. Many of the dowager's cronies were surprised and pleased to learn of her unexpected return to Town, and as a result Sir Harry was forced to exchange the warmest of greetings with people whom he had never seen in his life. Until this moment he had not considered the possibility that he might create a scandal by unintentionally giving someone the cut direct. By the time they had completed a circuit about the lobby, he welcomed the opportunity to return to the box. Lord Mannerly might await there, but Sir Harry discovered that he vastly preferred the known danger to the unknown.

"I vow the exercise has done me a world of good, Miss Darby," declared the *faux* Lady Hawthorne at last. "Shall we return to the others?"

Olivia giving her assent, they turned their steps in the direction of the boxes. They were almost within sight of their goal when Sir Harry—or rather his grandmother—was hailed by an elderly gentleman in an old-fashioned satin frock coat and knee breeches.

"Lady Hawthorne!" cried this worthy, hurrying to her side as quickly as the crowded condition of the lobby would allow. "Lady Hawthorne, as I live and breathe!"

Here, at least, was a face Sir Harry knew, for he had met Colonel Gubbins only that morning.

"Colonel Gubbins, is it really you? How long has it been?"

"Far, far too long, my dear Lady Hawthorne!" Having seized Sir Harry's gloved hands, the colonel showed no inclination to relinquish them. "I vow you haven't changed a bit. Still as lovely as ever!"

"La, sir, you flatter me," trilled Sir Harry, trying to retrieve his hands from the colonel's grasp.

"Not a bit! Imagine my delight when this charming young lady told me you were in town. When she let fall that you would be at the theater tonight, I came with the express hope of renewing your acquaintance. Where are you staying, if I may be so bold?"

"Why, at Grillon's, of course," replied Sir Harry, improvising rapidly.

"And may I have your permission to call upon you there?"

Not knowing how to answer, Sir Harry sought refuge in indignation. "Why, Colonel, I cannot think it proper for a gentleman to call upon a lady at her hotel!"

"Not for a schoolroom miss, perhaps, but for a woman of the world, such as yourself—"

"Fie on you, Colonel, you just said I had not aged a bit! Come along, Miss Darby, or we shall miss the second act."

"But—but—"

Colonel Gubbins was still "butting" as Sir Harry took Olivia's arm and steered her resolutely down the corridor to Lord Mannerly's box. For her part, Olivia had listened in some amusement to the exchange between her elderly companion and Colonel Gubbins. In spite of Lady Hawthorne's eccentricities, Olivia could not deny a certain fondness for the dowager; she supposed it must be due to that lady's marked resemblance to Sir Harry.

"Why I do believe you have acquired an admirer, my lady," she said, casting a mischievous glance at her companion.

"Hmph!" was the dowager's only reply.

It was almost midnight before Lord Mannerly's carriage rolled to a stop before the Hawthorne family's town house. The marquess handed the ladies down, and the front door was flung open to receive them. However, it was not Coombes, the butler, who greeted their arrival, but a distraught Mrs. Darby.

"Oh, Lady Hawthorne, thank God you have come!" she cried, twisting the fine cambric handkerchief she held in her twitching fingers. "I hate to impose on your ladyship's kindness—still, you must see how it is—quite unexpected, poor girl—if it were not an emergency—"

"Mama, what is it?" asked Olivia, interrupting this disjointed litany.

"A groom has just arrived from Clairmont with a message from your sister Liza," said her mother, sobbing lustily into the twisted scrap of cambric. "Her baby is coming early, and George is in Yorkshire, of all God-forsaken places! I must go to her at once! You won't mind staying with the girls, will you, Lady Hawthorne? It is your family's house, after all. Dear Lady Hawthorne! I knew I could count on you! You are truly all that is generous! Thank you, thank you!"

She continued in this strain for several minutes, never pausing long enough to allow Sir Harry to raise any objections to his new rôle as duenna. Then she hurried back into the house, announcing her intention of packing a portmanteau and departing within the hour, secure in the knowledge that her dear girls were safe in Lady Hawthorne's tender care.

Sir Harry stood motionless in the street, staring up at his town house as the realization dawned that he, still incognito, would now be sharing it with his fiancée.

# 6

Nor take her tea without a strategem.
EDWARD YOUNG, *Love of Fame*

When at last Sir Harry was sufficiently roused from his stupor to follow Mrs. Darby inside, he found the elegant entry hall in a state of chaos. Servants scurried up and down the curved staircase, some engaged in the packing of Mrs. Darby's belongings while others busied themselves in preparing a bedchamber for their unexpected guest. In the midst of all this turmoil, Olivia remained the personification of calm efficiency.

"I am sure you must be familiar with the layout of the house, Lady Hawthorne," she said, crossing the hall to stand beside him. "Mama has placed you in the front bedchamber, since Georgina assures us that it is your favorite. Georgina has the room next to yours, and I am in the back bedroom."

Sir Harry nodded, grateful to Georgina for placing as much distance as possible between his room and Olivia's. It seemed his younger sister had more intelligence than she had previously led anyone to believe.

"Of course," Olivia continued, "you will wish to have your things brought over from your hotel. You are staying at Grillon's, I believe? I shall send a footman over at once." And she prepared to suit the word to the deed, raising a hand in summons as a strapping lad descended the stairs with Mrs. Darby's trunk braced against his shoulder.

"No, no, that is not at all necessary," protested Sir Harry in real alarm. "Only let me pen a note to my grandson, and I—that is, I am sure dear Harry will see to everything."

Seeing nothing amiss in this request (save an overly optimistic opinion of Harry's capabilities which could, in Miss Darby's judgment, be ascribed to a doting grandmother's fondness for the grandson so clearly stamped with her own likeness), Olivia yielded to the dowager's request, leading Lady Hawthorne to the sitting room, where she produced paper and a quill from a delicate Sheraton writing table.

Sir Harry, taking pen in hand, was seized by a sudden fear that Olivia would discover him by his handwriting. The subsequent recollection that his letters to her had been sporadic and, as a rule, brief filled him with a curious mixture of relief and guilt. His irregular correspondence made it unlikely that Olivia would recognize his undeniably masculine hand, although he could not deny that, had he been less neglectful during the early stages of his courtship, he might have had no need for subterfuge now.

Shaking these self-recriminations aside, he scribbled a brief but explicit message, underscoring certain words for emphasis. Then, pronouncing this model of the epistolary art complete, he shook sand over his handiwork, folded it so as to conceal its contents, and sealed it with red wax.

"See that it is given to Higgins, my—my grandson's valet," he instructed Charles, the footman.

Some two hours later, after the ladies had long since repaired to their beds, a knock fell upon the door at the rear of the house which was designated the servants' entrance. Coombes, having been instructed to await the arrival of this nocturnal visitor, flung open the door. As the newcomer stepped into the light, the butler's eyes bulged. A lifetime spent in domestic service had brought him in contact with many ladies' maids, but never had he beheld a specimen like the one who now stood before him. The creature's lanky form was swathed in ill-fitting skirts which barely reached the ankles. Furthermore, the servant had apparently made free with the dowager's cosmetics, for the lean cheeks were liberally stained with rouge. A cheap straw bonnet covered curls of an improbable yellow hue, from under which peeped strands of salt-and-pepper gray.

"Well," pronounced this vision, glaring at his mesmerized host, "are you going to stand there staring all night, man, or are you going to conduct me to her ladyship's chamber?"

"Of course, sir—ma'am," Coombes replied hastily, recalled to the responsibilities of his position. If the old lady wanted to smuggle her paramour into the house by putting him in petticoats, well, that was no business of his. Besides, he had always known the Quality were a strange lot. "Right this way."

The abigail followed Coombes up the back stairs to the first floor, then down a luxuriously carpeted corridor which could not disguise the fact that the lady's maid was possessed of a decidedly masculine tread. At last they paused before a paneled door at the end of the hall.

"Her ladyship's chamber," announced Coombes before beating a hasty retreat back to the servants' quarters to regale the housekeeper with a description of the dowager's peculiar servant.

Casting a furtive glance up and down the corridor and finding it empty, the abigail rapped sharply on the door. Upon being bade enter, she opened it, darted quickly inside, and shut it firmly behind her.

"Higgins, you look positively breath-taking," remarked Sir Harry, surveying his servant appreciatively. He had divested himself of his wig and his evening gown (albeit not without difficulty), and now sat at the foot of the bed wearing nothing but his breeches and a wide grin.

"You may well say so, sir," responded Higgins with an affronted sniff. "Ladies' maid, indeed! Just how long do you think you can keep up this charade, if I might ask?"

"As long as necessary," said Sir Harry with steel in his voice. "Until the day of my nuptials, if need be—upon which occasion I shall double your wages."

"And if the lady discovers the rig you're running and cries off?"

Sir Harry's grin faded, to be replaced by a worried frown. "Ah, Higgins, that don't bear thinking of!"

☙

On the day following the Covent Garden outing, Lord Mannerly paid a call on his maternal aunt, the dowager duchess of Ramsey. Upon reaching her residence in Grosvenor Square, he was met by a butler who was starchier than his uncle, the late Duke, ever had been. This awe-inspiring personage conducted him to the Chinese Saloon, where her Grace was receiving.

His mother's elder sister, although on the shady side of sixty, still retained her slender figure, and although her fair complexion was marred by the faintest of lines about her eyes and mouth, her exquisite bone structure guaranteed the sort of beauty that age cannot destroy. Her present surroundings complemented her personal attractions, for the red satin wall coverings and black lacquer *chinoiserie* furnishings called attention to her delicate beauty.

"Forgive me, Aunt Augusta," said the marquess, kissing her cheek.

"I see it has been far too long since I called. The last time I was here, this room was Egyptian."

"I know you did not come to admire the furniture, Selwyn," remarked the duchess, as her nephew weighed a fat Buddha in his hand.

Lord Mannerly replaced the Buddha figure with a shudder. "Quite right. I cannot share our Prince's fondness for the Oriental style."

"Unhandsome! If you persist in insulting my taste, nephew, I shall be forced to ring for tea."

"That would indeed be adding insult to injury. As if it were not punishment enough that you expect me to sit on these unnatural chairs—my dear aunt, what do you call them?"

"That is a *klismos* chair, Selwyn, as if you did not already know," replied the duchess with asperity.

"Indeed? And I thought the *klismos* was Greek. I must call on you more often, Aunt. These visits are so educational, are they not?"

Ruthlessly, her Grace of Ramsey tugged the bell pull and ordered the butler to bring in the tea tray. Thus chastised, her recalcitrant nephew lapsed into silence.

"Now, Selwyn, to what do I owe the honor of this visit? And do not give me any nonsense about education, for I know very well that you think you know everything already."

"Oh, but I do not," protested the marquess. "And that is why I seek the benefit of your vast storehouses of information. What can you tell me about the dowager Lady Hawthorne, relict of a Leicestershire baronet?"

"Lady Hawthorne," echoed the duchess pensively, casting her mind back over the decades past. "What do you wish to know?"

"I have no idea. I only hope I will recognize it when I hear it."

"Well, if memory serves, she was several years older than I—"

"Everyone is older than you, dearest, including your own daughter," put in Mannerly.

"Flatterer! As I recall, she was the daughter of a viscount, Langford, I believe—yes, I'm sure of it. She had very much the look of the family, poor dear, and although the Langford men were generally accounted a handsome lot, their features did not sit well on a feminine countenance. If she produced any female descendants, I pity them."

"You may reserve your pity for those who need it," her nephew informed her. "Lady Hawthorne's granddaughter is a diamond of the first water."

Her Grace's eyebrows rose, her interest piqued. "Indeed? Sits the wind in that quarter?"

Lord Mannerly gave a snort of derisive laughter. "Acquit me, I beg you, of having designs on a chit barely out of the schoolroom! Actually, I find Miss Darby, the fiancée of the current baronet, of far greater interest."

The duchess bent a frown of disapproval on her errant nephew.

"Selwyn, you would not make advances to a woman who is already spoken for!"

"Do you know me so little, Aunt? Of course I would!"

Her Grace gave a musical laugh. "I have always had a weakness for a rake, Selwyn. I suppose that is why I tolerate you." Her smiles turned to frowns as a new thought struck her. "She is not a Long Meg, is she, this granddaughter? Lady Hawthorne was taller than is pleasing in a female, although where she got her height remains a mystery, for the Langfords are not much above the average."

"No, no Long Meg. Now, what else can you tell me about Lady Hawthorne?"

The duchess shrugged her frail shoulders. "Not much, I'm afraid, except that she has resided in Bath for the last twenty years or more."

"'Resided' being the operative word," put in her nephew. "She has recently taken up residence in London—Curzon Street, to be exact."

"Indeed? Well! Now I am the one being educated! Shall I call on her, do you think?"

Lord Mannerly hesitated. If there were anything havey-cavey about Lady Hawthorne, his aunt would be the one to spot it. "I should be eternally grateful if you would do so."

The duchess raised a skeptical eyebrow. "*That*, Selwyn, I should like to see!"

# Miss Darby's Duenna

The morning sun rose high over the city of Bath, casting a golden hue over the local limestone which comprised its stately Georgian architecture. Although no longer the fashionable resort it had once been, the city still had a distinguished, if somewhat dated, air, not unlike the many elderly aristocrats who lingered there in fond recollection of their younger days. Numbered among these venerable denizens was the dowager Lady Hawthorne. From her lodgings in Laura Place, this worthy gentlewoman frowned at the view which had greeted her virtually every morning for the past twenty years.

"Draw the curtains, Mildred," she ordered her companion, a thin, colorless woman of indeterminate age. "The sunlight will fade the carpet."

"Yes, my lady."

Miss Mildred Hunnicutt scurried to do her employer's bidding, grateful for the quirk of fate which had made her second cousin to a widow of wealth and position, and thus provided her with genteel employment and a roof over her head. Alas, fate was not often kind to spinster ladies, and Miss Hunnicutt had abandoned all matrimonial hopes many years earlier, when her sweetheart had married a young woman chosen by his family while the bridal couple were still in their respective cradles.

Having carried out Lady Hawthorne's command, Miss Hunnicutt

returned to the table where the dowager sat scanning the newspaper as she sipped her morning chocolate. Knowing that her ladyship detested interruptions, Miss Hunnicutt held her tongue as she buttered a slice of toast. As the silence lengthened, the companion thought longingly of the Gothic romance she had recently borrowed from the lending library and wished she might return to her room to fetch it. But alas, Lady Hawthorne was no more fond of novels than she was of interruptions. In fact, as Miss Hunnicutt recalled, the last time she had seen her employee thus indulging, she had insisted on presenting her with an uplifting volume of sermons to read in its stead. Recalling this incident, the companion suppressed a sigh and contented herself with perusing the back of Lady Hawthorne's newspaper.

While it made a poor substitute for the thrilling works of Mrs. Radcliffe, the page presenting itself to Miss Hunnicutt contained the society news from London, and so she passed the time in learning the latest doings of the *beau monde*, their identities thinly veiled by the lavish use of initials and abbreviations. She had spent several minutes thus agreeably occupied when one tidbit surprised a startled squeak from her lips.

"Well, Mildred?" demanded Lady Hawthorne impatiently, lowering her newspaper to frown at her errant employee. "I trust you will explain why you saw fit to interrupt this fascinating account of Lord Mablethorpe's sojourn to America? I had just reached the part where his party was set upon by savages."

"I beg your pardon, my lady," Miss Hunnicutt twittered, "but I found this item most interesting. Tell me, is Sir Harry not betrothed to a Miss Darby?"

"Miss Darby, Miss Derwood, something like that. Although why any woman of sense would choose to marry my ramshackle grandson quite escapes me. Impudent young popinjay! Although I must confess, the lad is as handsome as he can stare," she added with a glance toward the mantle, where a yellowed miniature revealed a curly-haired boy cradling a redheaded infant on his lap. "Indeed, I have often detected in his countenance a pronounced resemblance to myself."

"I have often remarked upon it also, my lady," replied Miss Hunnicutt dutifully, thankful to be spared a scolding.

"But that is neither here nor there," continued Lady Hawthorne brusquely. "Why do you bring up my grandson now, when I was so enjoying reading of Lord Mablethorpe's travels?"

"I beg your pardon, my lady, but I thought you might find this item of interest." She reached for the dowager's newspaper, then hesitated. "With your permission, of course."

"Oh, very well," agreed Lady Hawthorne with obvious reluctance.

Miss Hunnicutt turned the paper over and began to read aloud. "'The dowager Lady H. has recently returned to the Metropolis after a prolonged residence in Bath. Lady H., grandmother of Sir H. H., was seen at Covent Garden with her granddaughter Miss H., Lord M., and Miss D., who is rumored to be betrothed to Sir H. Can it be wedding bells which have lured Lady H. out of seclusion?'" Lowering the newspaper, Miss Hunnicutt regarded her employer expectantly.

"What of it, Mildred?" asked Lady Hawthorne, unimpressed.

"Is it not extraordinary, my lady? Why, it could have been describing you!"

"Indeed it could have, were it not for one minor detail: it says Lady H. has recently returned to London, and I, you will observe, am still very much in Bath."

"Still, it is unusual, you must own," persisted the companion.

"Nonsense! Why, there must be any number of dowagers in London with the same initials, and I'll wager most of them have grandsons. Now, unless you can find something worthwhile to say, kindly let me finish my article in peace."

"Yes, my lady," murmured Miss Hunnicutt, quite cowed.

ଔ

While in Bath Lady Hawthorne perused Lord Mablethorpe's account of his American travels, readers of the London newspapers were made privy to the information that Lady Clairmont had presented her husband with a son and heir, and that both mother and child were doing well. These happy tidings (which had been delivered to Curzon Street by messenger on the evening after Mrs. Darby's hasty departure) were gladly received by all who had known Mrs. Darby's eldest daughter before her marriage to the viscount. The predictable result was a steady stream of morning callers to Curzon Street. Upon their arrival, the visitors discovered that the new grandmother had gone to assist at her daughter's lying-in, and that Miss Hawthorne's grandmother, recently of Bath, had taken on the rôle of duenna.

Happy as she was for her sister, the new aunt, Miss Darby, found her sudden celebrity something of a trial. She endured her visitors' congratulations with a strained smile, but found it harder to answer with equanimity their coy suggestions that she would soon be the one marrying and setting up her nursery. For as plentiful as her callers were, the one she most wanted to see was conspicuously absent. Her heart leaped every time the door knocker sounded, only to plummet when the butler announced someone other than Sir Harry.

But, Olivia told herself, she did not care. If Harry did not wish for her company, there was another who did. Indeed, had it not been for Lord Mannerly, she did not know how she would have managed. The marquess was as attentive as Harry was neglectful, and his obvious admiration was a balm to her wounded pride. He had called in Curzon Street on the morning following the birth announcement, accompanied by his aunt, the duchess of Ramsey.

"I understand your sister has given birth to a boy," said Lord Mannerly as he bowed over her hand. "Allow me to tell you that I have never seen a maiden aunt more lovely."

"I'll wager you say that to all the young ladies," scolded Miss Darby playfully, her cheeks nevertheless turning pink with pleasure.

"Tell me, Miss Darby, what has Sir Harry to say to your sister's happy news? I daresay he looks forward to the day when he can set up his own nursery."

At the mention of her absentee bridegroom, Olivia lost her rosy glow. "I have seen little of Harry of late, my lord. He stays very busy, you see."

"Perhaps his loss may be my gain. I realize I must be a poor substitute for the man you are promised to marry, but I should be honored to offer you my services as an escort. Do you like horses, Miss Darby? I have a fine pair of blacks which I exercise regularly in the park. I should be pleased if you would accompany me."

"I should like that very much," replied Olivia, her spirits lifting somewhat.

"I shall call for you at four," promised the marquess, then rose to join his aunt.

The duchess of Ramsey, in the meantime, had been renewing her long-neglected acquaintance with Lady Hawthorne. Shortly after being reintroduced to the dowager, her Grace had been seized by the conviction that her nephew's suspicions were well-founded, although she could not have said precisely what had drawn her to such a conclusion. Certainly Lady Hawthorne's looks had altered greatly since the last time she had seen her, and yet the duchess was not so vain as to suppose the passing of twenty years had left her own visage untouched by Time.

Nor did Lady Hawthorne's conversation provide any clues. The duchess asked several probing questions concerning the various members of Lady Hawthorne's family, and she had been given an equal number of innocuous replies. Still, she could not shake the conviction that something was not quite right.

The subject of Lady Hawthorne's family led not unnaturally to a discussion of her home in Bath, and the numerous mutual acquaintances who had flocked to that once-fashionable spa to take the waters. Here the duchess found Lady Hawthorne less loquacious, and here she found the opening she sought.

"Tell me, Lady Hawthorne," she said, pausing to take a sip of tea from her delicate Sèvres cup, "do you ever see Lady Thurston-Whyte? I understand her physician advised her to take the cure last year."

The dowager was in the process of selecting a seed cake from the tray, but at the duchess's unexpected question, this confection crumbled in her fingers, raining crumbs onto her plate. "Lady Thurston-Whyte?" she echoed. "You must know, your Grace, that I do not get about as much as I did in my younger days. But now that you mention it, I believe I have occasionally encountered Lady Thurston-Whyte in the Pump Room."

"Indeed?" was the duchess's response.

In the next instant, Lord Mannerly came to collect his aunt, and the subject was dropped as the pair bid their hostess farewell.

Upon seeing Lord Mannerly vacate his post, Georgina claimed the marquess's place beside Olivia on the sofa, from which vantage point she observed through narrowed eyes as he exchanged pleasantries with the *faux* Lady Hawthorne.

"Tell me, Olivia, what do you think of him?" Georgina asked.

"Lord Mannerly? I think he is quite the most charming man I have ever met."

"There are some," said Georgina with a show of indifference, "who consider Harry charming."

"Oh, Harry is not lacking in charm, when he chooses to exercise it. But," added Olivia, her magnificent eyes sparkling with mischief, "Harry is the sort of gentleman one marries. Lord Mannerly is the sort with whom one enjoys a shocking flirtation."

Georgina lost no time in reporting this remark to her brother, after which she requested permission to inform the Reverend Mr. Collier of the birth of Mrs. Darby's first grandchild. Permission being granted, Georgina tripped lightly from the room in search of writing paper, sent on her way with Sir Harry's rather grimly expressed hope that his sister's courtship would be more successful than his own.

Alas, but such was not the case. Georgina had no sooner dipped quill to inkwell than she discovered the good vicar's face mysteriously erased from her memory. Oh, she well remembered his blue eyes, golden curls, and aristocratic brow. But when she tried to assemble these pleasing characteristics into a unified whole, the beloved countenance remained maddeningly elusive. Instead, the marquess's black eyes and mocking smile swam before her as if permanently engraved on the pressed vellum. Georgina stared at this image for a long moment, until a drop of ink dripped from her quill, marring the crisp white writing paper with a large black blot. Georgina crumpled the ruined sheet into a ball and threw it into the grate.

"Well, Aunt Augusta?" prompted the marquess as soon as they had quit Curzon Street.

"You are quite right, Selwyn," pronounced the duchess. "I do not know who that woman is, but she is certainly not Lady Hawthorne—at least, not the Lady Hawthorne I knew."

"Aha!"

The duchess gave a derisive snort. "The woman told me she occasionally met Lady Thurston-Whyte in the Pump Room! Of all the taradiddles!"

"I feel sure I shall regret asking, but what makes you so certain it was a taradiddle?"

"Look up Lord Thurston-Whyte in *Debrett's*, my boy," advised his aunt. "There is not, to my knowledge, any such peerage in all Britain."

# 7

Oh, what a plague is love! How shall I bear it?
She will inconstant prove, I greatly fear it.
ANONYMOUS, *Phillida Flouts Me*

To Sir Harry, it seemed as if his life had become a nightmare from which he could not awaken. His morning had been spent doing the pretty to an endless stream of morning callers, all the while watching out of the corner of his eye as Olivia flirted with his nemesis in a manner which could only be described as brazen. His evening promised to be no better, as he was committed to escort Olivia and Georgina to Vauxhall Gardens, where he would no doubt be forced to dance attendance on his sister while Lord Mannerly steered Olivia down various dark and secluded walks. For herein lay the fatal flaw in his ill-conceived plan: while he in his new persona could certainly keep Miss Darby under his watchful eye, the *faux* Lady Hawthorne could do nothing to further his own courtship. In assuming his disguise, Sir Harry had unwittingly given the marquess a clear field, having effectively removed himself as a rival.

A rival. . . Sir Harry stroked his jaw, disconcerted as always at finding it clean-shaven. A rival. . . If someone else were to court Olivia, someone who could spike Mannerly's guns without being a threat to Olivia's heart. . . .

The idea, having lodged itself in his brain, took root and blossomed. Sir Harry cast about in his mind for a suitable swain for his intended, then penned a brief missive to the Honourable Felix Wrexham.

Mr. Wrexham, upon receiving this epistle, could not fathom why the dowager Lady Hawthorne, whom he had never met, should suddenly require his presence; even less did he understand why she should insist that he come alone. Nevertheless, Mr. Wrexham had a healthy respect for his elders, and so he followed his instructions to the letter, presenting himself at the front door not more than an hour after receiving his summons.

It being Coombes's half-day, Mr. Wrexham was ushered into her ladyship's presence by John, a wide-eyed footman who had heard the other servants gossiping about the dowager's "lady's maid," and had not believed the half of it. In fact, he had suggested to the upstairs maid, with whom he was walking out, that Coombes was exaggerating to make a better tale, but now it appeared the butler had understated the case. It seemed the old girl had more than one lover on her string, this one Quality-born and less than half the old lady's age, beside! Flinging open the door to the front drawing room, John announced the visitor, then hurried back to the kitchen to regale the rest of the staff with this newest discovery.

Meanwhile Mr. Wrexham, unaware of the stir he was causing belowstairs, bowed over the dowager's hand. "'Servant, my lady," he said. "Happy to be of service any way I can."

"You can be of service by giving my hand back, you gudgeon!" replied Sir Harry, jerking his hand free before Mr. Wrexham could press a kiss onto it.

"*Harry*?" uttered Mr. Wrexham incredulously. "What the—"

"Shhh! D'you want to inform the entire household?"

"But the wig, the dress! Dash it, Harry, what's toward?"

"It's a long story, I'm afraid. I shall tell you in a minute, but first I must know if I can trust you. Will you help me, Felix?"

"Do anything I can," promised Mr. Wrexham. "What do you want me to do?"

"I want you to court Miss Darby."

At this declaration, Mr. Wrexham's jaw dropped, and he gaped at his host in a manner unflatteringly reminiscent of a fish.

"Close your mouth, Felix, before something flies into it," recommended Sir Harry.

Mr. Wrexham shut his mouth, swallowed hard, and found his tongue at last. "Now, look here, Harry, don't think you can palm your bride off on me, for I won't—"

But he got no further. Sir Harry, despite his petticoats, launched himself from his chair and, seizing the unfortunate Mr. Wrexham by his cravat, hauled him to his feet. "Watch how you speak of Miss Darby, Felix, or I'll call you out!"

"But you don't wish to marry her, do you?" rasped Mr. Wrexham through Sir Harry's viselike grip on his throat. "I mean, it ain't like you love the girl."

Mr. Wrexham's words struck Sir Harry with all the force of a thunderbolt. Not love Livvy? Not love the girl whose fierce devotion had once prompted her to follow him all over the Home Wood on that blasted pony? Whose sweet femininity had once provided a welcome change from the all-male bastions of first Eton and then Oxford? Whose white shoulders and bosom were even now driving him insane with jealousy and unfulfilled longing?

What a fool he had been! He had loved her all his life, and had not known it until now, when it appeared as if he might lose her.

"What about Violetta?" Mr. Wrexham's voice seemed to come from far away. "Thought you loved her."

With a snort of derision, Sir Harry released his grip on his friend's neck. "Violetta was nothing more than a schoolboy's fantasy. Olivia I shall love until the day I die—which might come sooner than expected, for if I lose her to that loose screw Mannerly, well, I shall be forced to put a bullet through my brain."

Mr. Wrexham, while acknowledging that Miss Darby was a deuced pretty girl, was at a loss to explain his friend's sudden preference for her slender beauty over Violetta's more robust charms. However, Sir Harry's sinister conclusion wrested his attention away from fond recollections of the actress's physical attributes and back to the business at hand.

"Here now, Harry, no need to act rashly," protested Mr. Wrexham. "Mannerly ain't won yet, you know. Miss Darby is still your fiancée, and all that. You'll come out all right. Do anything I can to help you."

"Will you, indeed?"

Mr. Wrexham, seeing his friend's kindling eye, knew a moment's uncertainty. Still, a gentleman never went back on his word. "Course I will. Just name it."

Sir Harry leaned forward in his chair. "I have a plan," he began.

Mr. Wrexham's intelligence was not swift, but after Sir Harry had recited his tale two or three times, he had a commendable grasp of the plot and his rôle in it. To this he voiced only one objection.

"But what if she—er—"

"Yes, Felix? What is it?"

The tips of Mr. Wrexham's ears turned a delicate rose hue. "What if Miss Darby conceives a *tendre* for me? Shouldn't like to toy with a lady's affections. Not at all the thing."

But Sir Harry's estimation of his friend's charms was not so high. "Don't be a gudgeon, Felix," he advised. "Do you honestly think any female would favor your attentions over the marquess of Mannerly's?"

"No. At least, Violetta don't."

"Quite right," said Sir Harry.

ᘓ

While Sir Harry plotted with Mr. Wrexham, Olivia, accompanied by Georgina and the maid who served both young ladies, perused the shops of Bond Street in search of a ribbon in just the right shade to match her best carriage dress. Her diligence was rewarded at Grafton House, where she found the elusive hue at such a bargain price that she was also able to purchase a modish new reticule in the shape of an Etruscan vase.

In point of fact, Olivia was looking forward to her drive with the marquess far more than was seemly for a young lady who was pledged to wed another. By the time Lord Mannerly called in Curzon Street, she had spent an inordinate amount of time before her looking glass, indulging in an activity which in a vainer female would have been called preening. Nor were her efforts in vain, for Lord Mannerly, handing her up into his curricle, was moved to declare that he had never seen her in better looks.

"How unhandsome of you, my lord," scolded Olivia, giving his sleeve a playful tweak. "For if you have never seen me look better, I can only assume that I normally look worse."

"Your assumption is incorrect, Miss Darby," responded the marquess, guiding his cattle into the flow of traffic. "Your appearance never fails to please, and this consistency is a great part of your charm."

"I shall strive to maintain the precedent I have set, my lord," vowed Olivia solemnly, then laughed aloud in the pure pleasure of being young and female and admired by a man.

Lord Mannerly joined in her laughter, and it was a merry pair which entered the gates of St. James Park. Mannerly, it seemed, knew everyone, and they frequently paused in their circuit about the park so that the marquess might greet some acquaintance, many of whom begged to be introduced to his fair companion.

But of Sir Harry there was no sign, and Olivia's pleasure in her newfound popularity soon palled. Lord Mannerly, sensing her sudden change of mood, surmised the reason, and judged it time to make his first move. He suggested that they stroll about the Mall for awhile, and, receiving a reply in the affirmative, tossed the reins to his tiger and descended from the vehicle. Then, taking Olivia firmly by the waist, he lifted her down from the curricle and set her on her feet, allowing his hands to remain at her waist the merest fraction of a second longer than necessary before taking her hand and drawing it through the crook of his arm.

Olivia, startled by this sustained contact, was not sure which she found most disturbing: the contact itself, or the little shudder of pleasure which coursed through her body at the marquess's touch. Hoping to cover her confusion, she fixed the marquess with a bright, false smile which, had she but known it, informed him of her feelings quite as plainly as if she had spoken them aloud.

"I vow, my lord," she said with forced cheerfulness as they set out on foot across the grass, "it appears all the world is in the park today."

"It certainly appears that way," agreed Lord Mannerly, leading her slowly but inexorably in the direction of a stone bench screened from public view by a high hedge. "And yet, I can think of at least one member of the *ton* who is missing."

A delicate blush stained Olivia's cheeks. "If you refer to Harry, my lord, he has many interests in Town. I am sure he cannot wish to dance attendance on his fiancée every minute."

"The more fool he," replied the marquess promptly. "If his other interests command so much of his time, perhaps he would do better not to embark upon the sea of holy matrimony just yet."

Olivia looked up, her pride stung by Mannerly's insinuation. "You think he should not have asked me to marry him?"

"On the contrary, Miss Darby, I think you deserve better." Having reached his destination, he drew her down to sit beside him on the bench. "Beauty such as yours, my dear, deserves to be admired, to be cherished by a man. By the *right* man," he amended, snaking his arm about her waist.

"I hardly think this c-conversation is p-proper, my lord," stammered Olivia, all too aware of the nearness of the marquess and the telltale pounding of her own heart.

"Not 'my lord,' Miss Darby. My name is Selwyn."

"I am sure H-Harry would not l-like—"

"Harry is not here," Mannerly reminded her. "Try it: Selwyn. Sel-wyn."

"S-Sel-w-wyn," echoed Olivia shakily.

"Very good. Now try it again," said the marquess, lowering his head to hers. "Sel-wyn."

"S-Sel—" Lord Mannerly's movement caused Olivia to look up, and once her eyes fixed with his, she found it impossible to look away. Like a rabbit confronted by a cobra, she stared transfixed as his lips, still forming his name, descended to meet hers.

But whether Olivia would have surrendered to the marquess's embrace would never be known, for in the same instant that his lips reached hers, he was hailed by a newcomer.

"Well met, Mannerly," cried this worthy, a young man whose saffron yellow pantaloons and inordinately high shirt-points proclaimed him a budding Tulip. "Heard you was returned from the Continent. That is—" Mr. Wrexham broke off abruptly, recalling too late his friend's account of the reason for Mannerly's exile. "—What I mean is, fine time to see Paris and all that, now that Boney's no longer running tame."

Lord Mannerly raised his quizzing glass and inspected the unfortunate Mr. Wrexham with an expression which gave the younger man to understand that his presence was unwelcome. "Good day, Mr.—Wickham, isn't it?"

"Wrexham—Felix Wrexham, don't you know," replied that worthy, undaunted. "I say, Mannerly, won't you introduce me to your fair companion?"

"But of course," drawled the marquess, suddenly enlightened as to the artless Mr. Wrexham's intentions. "Miss Darby, may I present Mr. Wrexham, who is, I believe, the boon companion of your fiancé. Mr. Wrexham, Miss Darby."

"'Servant, Miss Darby," said Mr. Wrexham, making his bow to the red-faced young lady without whose affection his friend would consider life a burden. "Tell me, how d'you find Harry?"

Olivia had been understandably chagrined at having been discovered in a compromising position, particularly by an intimate of her betrothed, but Mr. Wrexham's seemingly innocuous question had the effect of recalling that young lady's grievances to her mind, and suddenly her own sins seemed the lesser by comparison.

"I find Harry quite well, sir, when I can find him at all," she replied with some asperity. "I daresay I shall see him at Almack's on

Wednesday, however. Tell me, Mr. Wrexham, do you go often to the Assembly Rooms?"

Mr. Wrexham shook his head, indicating the negative. Like most young blades, he felt nothing but revulsion for the King Street establishment which was as notorious for its exclusivity as it was for the stale cake and tepid lemonade which it habitually foisted upon its select clientele. "Can't abide the place, myself," he said, then, recalling his mission, added hastily, "that is, never cared for it until now. Should be honored, though, if you would stand up with me for the waltz, Miss Darby."

"I am sure the pleasure will be mine, sir," said Olivia with perhaps more civility than truthfulness.

ങ

It was a melancholy Mr. Wrexham who presented himself in Curzon Street later that afternoon. Although not a student of philosophy, he was well aware of mankind's innate tendency to kill the messenger when one disliked the message. And he was quite certain that Sir Harry would dislike this message very much, indeed. Upon being shown into her ladyship's presence by the goggle-eyed John, he accepted a glass of sherry and sat down in the chair nearest to the door, in case he should find it necessary to beat a hasty retreat. He then proceeded to recount the afternoon's events to an enthralled audience of one.

"And then," concluded Mr. Wrexham, setting down his wineglass and mentally measuring the distance to the door, "Mannerly leaned forward, like he was going to kiss her."

"Did she let him?" demanded Sir Harry, edging forward in his chair in anticipation of the answer. "More to the point, did she kiss him back?"

Mr. Wrexham shrugged. "Can't say. Thought it time to break up the *tête-à-tête*."

Sir Harry collapsed back in his chair, torn between disappointment at not knowing and relief at being spared the agony of hearing what he had not wanted to know. Unsure whether to berate his friend or thank him, he contented himself with cursing Lord Mannerly under his breath.

"There's only one thing for it, then," he declared at last. "I shall have to put in an appearance at Vauxhall tonight."

But Mr. Wrexham had no very high opinion of this plan. "Can't have thought, Harry," he said, shaking his head. "Be ruined if you're discovered. Blackballed from White's, and all that. And what of Miss Darby? Ruin her reputation, if the *ton* knew you and she'd been living under the same roof. No chaperone, you know, unmarried and all. Won't do."

"But I won't be discovered. I've pulled off this charade once already at Covent Garden, and this time it will be even easier, because you're going to help me."

"I am?"

"You are." Sir Harry refilled his glass with sherry, wishing he were brave enough to risk scandalizing the servants by ringing for a bottle of brandy for the dowager. Swirling the amber-colored liquid about in his goblet, he outlined a plan whereby he would enter the popular pleasure gardens in his Lady Hawthorne persona. He would then leave Olivia and Georgina to Mr. Wrexham's escort while he hastened to a waiting carriage, where Higgins would be waiting with his evening clothes. "Pity it ain't a masquerade night," he concluded with a sigh. "A domino would be a deuced sight easier to put on in the dark than a curst cravat."

# 8

Anger is a short madness.
HORACE, *Satires*

The party of four, escorted by Mr. Wrexham and including "Lady Hawthorne," Miss Hawthorne, and Miss Darby, arrived at Vauxhall Gardens via the water route along the Thames, it having the advantage of novelty as well as being safer than the entrance by land. Mr. Wrexham duly paid two shillings per person to allow them admittance, and soon the little group found itself in a fairy land of winking lanterns and tree-lined walkways ending in mysterious grottoes. Georgina demanded to see the Grand Cascade, and, Olivia echoing this sentiment, Mr. Wrexham offered an arm to each, while the *faux* dowager, seeing, as she said, her charges in such capable hands, elected instead to await the trio in one of the supper boxes along the Grand Walk.

Sir Harry watched until he lost sight of Olivia in the crowd, then hurried back toward the entrance to the gardens, where Higgins was supposed to be waiting with his evening gear in a hired carriage. He was almost within sight of his destination when he heard a voice hailing him in ardent tones. Turning, he saw Colonel Gubbins bearing down upon him, his corsets creaking under the strain.

"My dear Lady Hawthorne!" panted the colonel as he closed the distance between them. "An unexpected pleasure!"

"The pleasure is all mine," lied Sir Harry, submitting uneasily to having his gloved hand pressed to the colonel's lips. "But I must not keep you from your party—"

"Think nothing of it! No one else could possibly hold a candle to your delightful companionship, my lady," declared the devoted swain, tucking Sir Harry's hand into the crook of his arm. "May I show you the Grand Cascade?"

"Thank you, sir, but I have already had the pleasure," said Sir Harry, withdrawing his hand in spite of the colonel's best efforts to retain it.

"Perhaps you might prefer to promenade along the Grand Walk."

A move to recapture Sir Harry's hand accompanied this suggestion, but before the colonel could achieve success in this endeavor, he was interrupted by two of his cronies who were eager to locate a good vantage point from which to view the fireworks. Seizing the opportunity presented by this distraction, Sir Harry slipped away. Once outside the gates, he located the waiting vehicle and strode in its direction as quickly as his narrow skirts and fragile slippers would allow.

Alas, the area surrounding Vauxhall had sadly decayed since Mr. Tyers had established the popular pleasure garden, and while the elite amused themselves within, strumpets plied their wares and pickpockets searched the crowd for easy marks just outside the gate. In this rather disreputable environment, it was hardly surprising that an elderly woman with no visible protector should be accosted by a representative of London's criminal element. As Sir Harry made his way toward the waiting carriage, he felt a hand close about his arm. Turning in surprise, he found himself confronted by an unsavory individual with beady black eyes and dirty straw-colored hair under a dark knitted cap.

"Now, Granny," snarled this person through a mouthful of rotting teeth, "I wonders where ye might be goin' in such an 'urry. I'll be bound ye'd get there faster without the weight o' them sparklers draggin' ye down." So saying, he reached out a grimy hand in the direction of the diamonds at Sir Harry's throat.

Once his initial alarm had passed, Sir Harry had little fear for his safety. Having successfully repulsed Colonel Gubbins's amorous advances, he was not afraid of a common thief. He saw no sign of a weapon in the man's possession, and had no doubt the fellow lacked the courage to accost a gentleman, or indeed anyone who might be capable of fighting back. Judging the element of surprise to be his best defense, Sir Harry restricted himself, for the moment, to the rôle of a frightened old lady.

"Don't hurt me," he pleaded in terrified accents. "I'll give you anything you want, but pray don't harm an old woman."

"Yer necklace, then, and any other gew-gaws wot ye 'appen to 'ave on yer person."

Sir Harry reached up as if to unclasp the necklace, then balled his fist and delivered himself of a punishing blow to his assailant's mouth, to the further detriment of that individual's teeth. As the fellow crumpled to a heap on the ground, Sir Harry hurried to the designated rendezvous, where he found an anxious Higgins pacing back and forth before the carriage.

"Quickly, man," urged Sir Harry, as the pair entered the vehicle and closed the door.

"I had almost given you up, sir," declared the valet in quavering tones. "Is everything all right?"

"Quite all right, Higgins, but remind me to carry a heavy object in my reticule from now on."

"A heavy object, sir? Whatever for?"

"Self-defense," uttered Sir Harry cryptically.

With his valet's able assistance, he hastily divested himself of his dowager's attire, then donned his own clothes as quickly as was possible by the uncertain light of the carriage's sole lantern. The most difficult part of the proceedings, as he had predicted to Mr. Wrexham, was the cravat, Higgins's advanced case of nerves rendering his first three attempts useless. At length, however, the long-suffering valet was able to produce an effort which was, if not quite up to his usual standards, at least respectable, and Sir Harry sallied forth to woo his bride, at long last his own man.

Meanwhile, having exhausted the charms of the Grand Cascade, Mr. Wrexham escorted the ladies back to the now empty supper box.

"Why, where has Lady Hawthorne gone, do you suppose?" Olivia wondered aloud. She scanned the crowds, but although she saw no sign of Lady Hawthorne among them, she did recognize another familiar figure—a tall, masculine form in elegant evening attire, whose unexpected appearance caused Olivia's face to light up.

Mr. Wrexham also observed this gentleman's approach, but with considerably less enthusiasm. Remembering his promise to keep Sir Harry's fiancée out of Lord Mannerly's clutches, he quickly turned to Olivia.

"I say, Miss Darby, would you care to dance? Waltz, you know."

"Of course," replied Olivia, more out of courtesy than any real desire to be partnered by Mr. Wrexham. She allowed him to lead her onto the dance floor, confident that the marquess would seek her out before the evening was much farther advanced.

And so it happened that, by the time Lord Mannerly reached the supper box, he found Georgina its only occupant.

"Good evening, Miss Hawthorne," said the marquess, making his bow. "You do not dance, I see. Will you permit me to rectify this shocking omission?"

Up went Georgina's chin. "Thank you, my lord, but I have no liking for the waltz."

"Indeed?" Mannerly's eyebrows rose in mild surprise. "Why ever not?"

"I should think it would be obvious. The very idea of a lady and gentleman whirling about in a public embrace! It is immoral and indecent!"

The marquess nodded in understanding. "In other words, you never learned the steps."

Since she had, in the days before the vicar set her feet on a higher path, spent many hours perfecting the movements of the waltz, she could not allow this charge to go unchallenged. "Although I do not choose to practice them, my lord, I certainly have learned the steps!" Georgina cried, flushing hotly.

"Prove it."

"I—I beg your pardon?"

Lord Mannerly offered his arm. "If you have indeed learned the steps, then prove it. Dance with me."

"I will not!"

"Very well. You leave me no choice but to believe your moral posturings are simply the envious outpourings of one who has spent too many dances sitting along the wall."

This accusation was more than the former belle of Leicestershire could bear. "All right," she said haughtily, rising to her feet. "I'll waltz with you. But only once, mind you, and only to prove that I do know the steps!"

The marquess made no reply, but bowed his acquiescence and led her onto the floor. Here Georgina began to repent of her rash decision. She had certainly waltzed before, but as her prior partners consisted entirely of her brother, her dancing-master, and a handful of rural admirers, nothing in her previous experience had prepared her for the virile nearness of the marquess of Mannerly. His hand at her waist seemed to burn her flesh through the thin fabric of her gown, and she fancied she could almost feel his warm breath ruffling her hair. As he twirled her about the floor, it seemed to Georgina that her feet no longer touched the ground, but floated in mid-air. Yes, the waltz was every bit as sinful as she had supposed; she had just not expected immorality to be so very thrilling.

"There," said Lord Mannerly at last, when the final strains of the violins had faded into the night. "When you return to Leicestershire, you may inform your vicar that the waltz is not nearly so wicked as you were led to believe."

"What? Oh—oh, yes, of course," said Georgina, uncharacteristically subdued. Suddenly Leicestershire and the Reverend James Collier seemed very far away.

ଓ

Sir Harry returned to his party a short time later to find Olivia in the supper box along with Georgina and Mr. Wrexham, partaking of rack punch and paper-thin slices of ham. As he strode purposefully toward the box, she looked up and saw him. For a moment Sir Harry fancied that something leaped in her eyes, but he quickly dismissed this notion as a trick of the light, combined with his own wishful thinking.

"Why, Harry," she said with studied nonchalance, "fancy meeting you here! It has been a while, has it not?"

"Far too long," he agreed gallantly, raising her hand to his lips. "Please believe that nothing but the most pressing circumstances could have kept me from your side."

Olivia refrained from commenting on an assertion whose accuracy she had reason to doubt. "Your grandmama was just here, Harry," she informed him. "She will be sorry to have missed you."

"She is visiting with her cronies, no doubt," replied Sir Harry with a shrug.

"You have come just in time, Harry," chimed in Georgina, who had not been privy to her brother's plans, and had consequently been momentarily taken aback by his unexpected arrival. "The fireworks start soon, you know."

"Yes, Harry, did you come for the fireworks?" asked his betrothed, opening and closing her fan with restless fingers. "I understand the display is most impressive."

He shook his head. "How could I stare at artificial rockets when I might gaze instead into Olivia's eyes?"

"What fustian, Harry!" scolded Olivia, but her color rose, and she glanced away.

"Have we time for a stroll along the Grand Walk before the fireworks start, my love? We have much to catch up on."

Although she had long dreamed of hearing herself thus addressed, Olivia was unused to such endearments on Sir Harry's lips and found the experience oddly disconcerting in the light of his recent negligence. Not knowing quite how to respond, she elected to counter his gallantries with humor. "I thought you cared nothing for the fireworks," she reminded him.

"I don't," he replied. "But I thought you should dislike missing them."

"On the contrary, I find I would much prefer to take a stroll along the Grand Walk," she said, rising from her chair. Strange as his behavior might seem, Olivia reasoned, Harry was here at last, and she intended to seize the moment. Who knew how long it might be before he thought to seek her out again?

Sir Harry placed her silk shawl about her shoulders and offered her his arm. They made small talk as they traversed the Grand Walk, until Sir Harry steered Olivia abruptly down one of the narrower, darker paths which intersected the Grand Walk at regular intervals. Their seclusion reminded Olivia all too vividly of her near-disastrous *tête-à-tête* with Lord Mannerly, and she struggled to maintain a carefree mien.

"It—it was quite a surprise, seeing you here," Olivia said, feeling an urgent need to fill the silence that stretched out between them. "What brought you to Vauxhall tonight?"

"I came in the hope of seeing you," Sir Harry said simply.

He paused beneath the concealing boughs of a poplar tree, and Olivia suddenly realized that they were quite alone. A whistling sound overhead drew her attention, and she looked up to see an explosion of red and blue stars. The fireworks, it seemed, had begun, and everyone else had taken places elsewhere on the grounds, where the view was better.

"What—what nonsense! As if you could not see me any time you wished simply by calling in Curzon Street! It is, after all, your house."

"And will be yours someday," said Sir Harry, possessing himself of her hands. "I usually prefer to take lodgings in Stratton Street when in London. The town house held no attraction for me, until the day you came to live there."

"Cut line, Harry," advised his betrothed, twisting her hands free. "You have hardly called in Curzon Street more than twice since I came to London. Why do you persist in talking such fustian?"

Sir Harry, doing his best to play the devoted lover, was perhaps understandably offended by this question. "I see! When Lord Mannerly addresses you thus, he is charming, but when I do it, it is fustian!"

"What, pray, has Lord Mannerly to say to anything?" demanded Olivia, her face flaming in combined fury and shame.

"Aha! You blush at the mention of his name! Just because you have not seen me, madam, do not think that I have not heard! You are almost daily in his company, and the attentions he shows you are so marked that you cannot fail to attract the worst sort of notice. Why, all of London is abuzz!"

"If you do not trust me, sir, I wonder you should wish to marry me!"

"If you intend to play me false before the ring is even on your finger, I wonder it myself!"

Now that the hateful words were out, the betrothed pair could only stare speechlessly at one another, each horrified that the other had spoken in earnest. Olivia, seized by the sudden fear that Sir Harry was on the brink of breaking the engagement, interrupted before he could speak the words she did not want to hear.

"I wish to return to my party, sir!" she demanded.

"What? Is your future husband not to enjoy the favors you bestow so readily upon another?" Without waiting for an answer, Sir Harry pulled his intended bride ruthlessly into his arms and crushed his lips against hers. She did not struggle against his embrace (or perhaps she could not, so tight was his hold on her), but he could feel the pounding of her heart against his chest. The taste of her lips and the warmth of her slender form in his arms effectively robbed Sir Harry of his anger, and his kiss grew gentler. "Oh, Livvy," he groaned as his lips traced the long-familiar yet unexplored planes of her face. So intent was he upon this exercise that he unwittingly loosened his hold on Olivia—whereupon she wrested herself free and administered a stinging slap to his cheek. Stunned into immobility, Sir Harry could only stare helplessly as his gentle bride turned and ran back up the path the way they had come.

Olivia, having won her freedom by violence, was dismayed to find it so very unwelcome. Too late, she discovered that it was better to be clasped in the arms of a livid Sir Harry than not to be so clasped at all. In her distress, and half-blinded by tears, she took a wrong turn and soon found herself quite lost, with no idea how to reach her party and no very clear recollection of the turns she had taken. It was in this condition that Lord Mannerly found her.

"Miss Darby!" called the marquess, picking up his pace so that he might fall into step beside her. "Is something the matter?"

"I—I seem to have lost my way," replied Olivia, valiantly blinking back the tears she did not want to be called upon to explain. She needn't have worried; Lord Mannerly took one look at her swollen lips and tumbled locks and formed a very accurate estimation of her evening's adventures. "Pray, my lord, will you escort me back to my party?"

Instead, Mannerly steered her to a stone bench recessed into a dark alcove. "Of course. But perhaps you had best rest here a moment and compose yourself."

"Y-you are very good, sir."

"Not at all," replied the marquess modestly, offering her his handkerchief. As Olivia dabbed at her eyes, Mannerly seated himself beside her and draped a comforting arm about her shoulders. "Now, Miss Darby, what has happened to upset you, and how may I be of service?"

"There is—nothing—that you can do," came the watery reply. "There is nothing anyone can do."

"Surely it is not so bad as all that!" chided the marquess gently, drawing her head down to rest on his shoulder. "Tell me the truth. Has Sir Harry been unkind?"

Olivia's only response was a sob, which Lord Mannerly understood to be a reply in the affirmative.

"There, there, my dear," he murmured into the dark curls tickling his chin. "There are other men, you know—men who would know how to cherish such an exquisite creature as yourself."

The marquess's words became kisses, whisper-soft kisses that trailed from the top of Olivia's head down to her ear. Olivia did not encourage his advances, but neither did she repulse them. After all, she reasoned (when she was capable of reason at all in the face of Mannerly's sweet onslaught), since she had already been tried and convicted, why should she not allow herself the luxury of committing the crime?

Sensing her surrender, the marquess stepped up the intensity of his assault. His mouth moved from her ear to the hollow of her throat, where Olivia's pulse beat tumultuously. Still meeting no resistance, he slowly bent her backwards.

Not until her back pressed against the hard, cold stone of the bench did Olivia come to her senses.

"I—I must return to my party," she protested for the second time that evening, as she struggled to sit upright.

If Mannerly was at all embarrassed, he gave no outward sign. Urbane as ever, he straightened his cravat and offered his arm to his mortified companion. "I am, as always, yours to command, my dear."

Inwardly, however, the marquess's emotions told a very different story. For perhaps the first time in his life, Lord Mannerly was completely nonplussed. The sundry other females of his acquaintance, from the buxom Drury Lane orange girl who had marked his coming of age to the notorious French comtesse who had relieved the monotony of his Parisian exile, had all parted with their rather dubious virtue with scarcely a backward glance. To be sure, his experience with women was wide and varied, but the seduction of a young lady of quality was a new undertaking for him, and one, it would seem, at which he was far from expert. To the marquess, the discovery of his own ineptitude was more disconcerting than the fact of Miss Darby's lack of response to his advances. The thought that Sir Harry Hawthorne might be his superior in matters concerning the fairer sex was so absurd that he dismissed it with a snort of derision, and yet the very idea that any woman might prefer that green youth to himself galled him beyond all bearing. Suddenly it was vitally important that he succeed in his seduction of Miss Darby. It was more than a matter of revenge; the reputation of the House of Mannerly was at stake.

# 9

When the wine goes in, strange things come out.
JOHANN CHRISTOPH FRIEDRICH VON SCHILLER, *Die Piccolomini*

Sir Harry, bereft of his love, lingered for some time alone in the secluded bower, idly pacing back and forth and shuffling his feet in a manner fatal to the beauty of his soft leather evening pumps. But Sir Harry was indifferent to such sartorial concerns. He had set out, at great risk to himself, to woo and win his lady and had ended by quarreling with her, receiving nothing but a very sore cheek for his pains. At last he roused himself from his reverie sufficiently to dispatch a lackey to Mr. Wrexham and the ladies, informing them that he had found his grandmother feeling unwell and was escorting her home.

Having accounted for the absence of both his personae, he set out to assuage his heartache by indulging in the usual vices favored by young men suffering the pangs of unrequited love. He proceeded to White's, where he drank too much brandy and wagered too much money at faro.

As one losing turn yielded to another, he waxed eloquent about the vagaries of the female mind and the folly of falling in love.

He was still engaged in "bucking the tiger" (albeit without much success) at three o'clock in the morning, when Lord Mannerly entered the gaming room. Sir Harry, seated with his back to the door, was unaware of the presence of his nemesis. Calling for another bottle in slurred accents, he placed his wager on the jack, and groaned when the exposed card was removed to reveal a queen.

"So close, and yet so far away," sighed a fellow player, a young officer whose own success at cards was only slightly greater than Sir Harry's. "But perhaps you are lucky at love instead."

Sir Harry, painfully aware of the angry red welt on his left cheek and vaguely sensing an insult through the fog of his inebriation, wheeled unsteadily about and seized his fellow gambler by the front of his scarlet coat. "And jusht—just—what do you mean by that, sirrah?"

The officer, who intended no insult, did not expect his expression of sympathy to be met with belligerence, and took umbrage at Sir Harry's rough handling of his person. "Why, only that your pile of vowels is almost as large as your pile of guineas was when you came in! Now, unhand me, you ruffian, before I draw your cork!"

Upon hearing this heated exchange, a small crowd gathered as gamblers all over the room abandoned their own games to watch the scene unfolding at the faro table. The older men were concerned with maintaining the dignity of their establishment; the younger men were primarily interested in getting a good view of the mill which seemed imminent. Only Lord Mannerly remained in his seat. Flicking open the lid of his enameled snuffbox, he placed a pinch of snuff on his wrist and raised it to his nose, inhaling deeply as he silently observed the proceedings.

"Damn it, I'll not have Livvy's name ban—bandied about this way!" declared Sir Harry, lurching to his feet.

"So you accuse me of dishonoring a lady, do you?" demanded the soldier. "Perhaps you would care to repeat the accusation over pistols at Paddington Green! Name your second, sir!"

"Come, Eversley, can't you tell when a man is half-seas over?" Mannerly did not even raise his voice, but the room fell silent the moment he spoke. "In his present condition, Sir Harry's opinions can be of no particular importance to you."

This seemed to satisfy the military gentleman, but Sir Harry took instant affront. "I am not—*hic*—drunk!" he asserted, unmindful of the empty bottle at his elbow. "I can hold my liquor with the best of 'em! Why, I—"

"Nonsense, boy, you are quite foxed," repeated the marquess.

"*I* am foxed? *You*, my lord, are the fox—in the hen house, no less! Well, she's mine—*hic*—do you hear? I won't stand for it, Mannerly!"

"Indeed, it is a wonder to me that you can stand at all," observed the marquess.

"I won't let Livvy's name be bandied about in pub—public!"

"Then, as you are the only one bandying names about, I suggest you take yourself home," replied the marquess in a voice that brooked no argument.

The other men moved aside to give Sir Harry access to the door. There was nothing he could do but gather the tattered remains of his dignity, along with the pile of vowels, and quit the room. As he stumbled noisily down the curved staircase to the ground floor, Lord Norville was moved to express the hope that the lad—a good sort, really, and not at all himself tonight—would reach his home without tumbling into the Thames.

"I shall see him home." Lord Mannerly rose from his chair, prepared to suit the word to the deed.

"In his present mood, I doubt he will wish for an escort," warned Norville. "He seems to fancy a grudge against you, Mannerly."

"He will never know I am there," promised the marquess, and quitted the room in Sir Harry's wake.

As soon as his footsteps faded away, the gaming room became a whirlwind of activity.

"A pony says Lord Mannerly beats Sir Harry to the altar with the Darby chit!" shouted one gamester above the hubbub.

"Make it a monkey!" said another.

"I'll cover that bet!" cried a third. "*Garçon*! The betting book!"

©

Sir Harry, unaware of the commotion he had left behind, staggered off in the direction of Curzon Street. Pools of feeble yellow light from the streetlamps penetrated the fog sufficiently to illuminate his way, although not so brightly as to reveal a second figure following at a discreet distance. Arriving at his town house, he tried the door and found it locked. He raised his cane to rap for Coombes to let him in, but some still-cognizant corner of his brain realized the folly of this action, and stayed his hand. Gradually it all returned to him: his disguise, the events at Vauxhall, and "Lady Hawthorne" supposedly asleep in her bed. No, he could not enter the house where he might be seen; to do so might raise questions, the answers to which would bring discovery, and with it disaster. Sir Harry stepped back to ponder the matter, applying all his powers of concentration (which, at that moment, were not much) to the problem.

The façade of his house jutted out some six feet beyond those of its immediate neighbors on either side, giving the house the benefit of a narrow side window on each floor in addition to those in the front and back. Beyond contributing to the window tax, these windows had the advantage of bringing sunlight into the rooms during the daylight hours, but at this particular time, Sir Harry was more interested in their potential for clandestine entrance. In keeping with the century-old fashion for *rus in urbe*, a large stone urn had been positioned in the corner formed by the adjoining walls, from whence sprang a stout ivy which climbed the wall to the roof.

Inspired, Sir Harry strode over to the urn, took hold of the ivy, and tugged with all his might. Upon finding that the plant would indeed support his weight, he removed his shoes, tucked them into the waistband of his breeches, and began to climb—a difficult feat for any man, but for one in his present inebriated condition, one nothing short of miraculous. He was perhaps some twelve feet off the ground when a slight sound from the street caught his attention. He looked down, and the sight of *terra firma* so far below was sufficient to shock him into a state approaching sobriety. However, he managed to maintain his hold on his leafy ladder, and at length reached the upper window. He rapped on it as loudly as he dared, and was soon rewarded by the sight of Higgins on the other side.

"Sir Harry!" cried his faithful servant. "Whatever are you doing out there, sir?"

"Trying to come inside, you nodcock! Open the window and let me in!"

Bobbing his head in agreement, Higgins threw open the sash and, seizing his master by the arm, dragged him over the casement. Sir Harry landed in a heap on top of his hapless valet, whereupon the shocked manservant uttered, "Sir, you reek of brandy!"

Sir Harry would have reiterated the claim that he could hold his liquor with the best of them, but the sound of a footstep in the hall recalled him to his purpose. "*Shhh*! See who is at the door, Higgins."

Higgins dragged the heavy brocade curtain across the open window, then shoved his master behind the drapery with such force that he almost knocked poor Sir Harry back out. Then, pausing only long enough to don his own wig and dressing gown, he crossed to the door just as a knock sounded on the other side of its paneled surface.

Sir Harry, watching from his hidden vantage point as Higgins opened the door, beheld a vision. Olivia wore a silk wrapper over her nightdress, her dark hair unbound and spilling over her shoulders in long, loose waves. Looking at her, Sir Harry felt an ache somewhere inside his chest, one that had nothing to do with the copious amounts of liquor he had poured down his gullet.

"Is something wrong, Higgins?" she asked. "I heard noises."

"Her ladyship is ill, miss," explained the servant.

"Shall I summon a physician?"

"No, no," was the quick reply. "I am sure he—she will feel much more the thing after a good night's sleep." And a pot of strong coffee, he added mentally.

"Very well, if you are sure," Olivia conceded reluctantly. "Still, if there is any change, do not hesitate to awaken me."

Higgins repeated his assurances that Lady Hawthorne would be quite all right, then gently but firmly closed the door. He listened for a moment to Olivia's retreating footsteps, then addressed his master.

"A close call, but I believe we got through that one rather well, didn't we, sir? Sir?"

But Sir Harry, sprawled unconscious before the window, made no reply.

ଔ

Lord Mannerly, having fulfilled his promise to Lord Norville by seeing Sir Harry safely home, was about to return to his own residence in Park Lane when Sir Harry's odd behavior gave him pause. From his vantage point across the street, he watched as that young man removed his shoes and began to scale the ivy clinging to the outside wall. A few moments later, he was treated to the sight of Sir Harry Hawthorne entering the Curzon Street town house through a window on the upper floor. Why, he wondered, might the head of the Hawthorne family find it necessary to enter his own house clandestinely? The question nagged at him all the way home. The answer, he was somehow sure, was important.

Upon reaching his own domicile, he poured himself a glass of sherry from the bottle awaiting him in the library, and sat in silence for a long while, staring into the flames dancing in the fireplace.

They were a strange lot, these Hawthornes, but what could one expect, with a stripling like Sir Harry as head of the family? A schoolroom chit who fancied herself a missionary, a dowager who until quite recently had lived the life of a recluse. . . .

A recluse? Mannerly had it on good authority that the dowager Lady Hawthorne had not left her Bath lodgings in twenty years or more. Why, then, would she suddenly take up residence in London just as Sir Harry's bride made her come-out? He remembered his curious impression of Lady Hawthorne that night at Covent Garden and his aunt's conviction that the old lady was not who she seemed, and his suspicions grew apace. It was interesting to recall that, as much as he had haunted Hawthorne House in recent weeks, he had never seen Sir Harry and his grandmother at the same time. Even tonight—*last* night, rather, at Vauxhall, Sir Harry had not arrived until after his grandmother had departed.

Of course! Why else should Sir Harry sneak into the window, unless he was already believed to be within? Furthermore, Sir Harry could hardly be seen entering the residence at such an hour, when all the world knew Miss Darby to have no other chaperone but the dowager Lady Hawthorne—who happened, most conveniently, to bear a marked resemblance to her grandson, and who walked, surprisingly enough, like a man.

Suddenly all the pieces of the puzzle fell neatly into place, and Lord Mannerly knew his long-awaited victory was at last within reach. He would have to call in Curzon Street the next morning to confirm his theory, but he was almost certain his surmise was correct. Refilling his wineglass, he raised it in a mock toast.

"Sir Harry Hawthorne, I salute you," he said aloud, addressing himself to the amber depths. "You have fought, and fought valiantly—but you have lost."

# 10

There is no disguise which can for long conceal love.
FRANÇOIS, DUC DE LA ROCHEFOUCAULD, *Reflections*

The following morning found Miss Georgina Hawthorne quite alone. Of her future sister-in-law Olivia there was no sign, although it was almost noon, and, judging from the anguished groan which emitted from her brother's room immediately after Higgins had entered milady's chamber to draw open the curtains, Georgina expected it would be quite some time before Sir Harry saw fit to make an appearance.

Thus left to her own devices, she found herself sunk in a fit of the dismals. In this frame of mind, she made a short breakfast of chocolate and toast, then applied herself to her daily perusal of the holy scripture. She had first begun these devotional readings upon her arrival in London, feeling sure that the reverend Mr. Collier would approve of this exercise as proof against the temptations of the social whirl. Unfortunately, in this aim it had failed miserably. Georgina found herself turning with alarming frequency to the Song of Songs, which is Solomon's. Indeed, so often had she turned to that most sensuous of books that her Bible now fell open to the page. She had, of course, neither the opportunity nor the inclination to discuss the matter with her vicar, but she suspected the reverend would find her new reading preferences even more objectionable than the Gothic novels he frequently denounced from the pulpit.

Heaving a discontented sigh, she closed the Bible and gazed out the window, where the gray skies and drizzling rain seemed perfectly matched to her mood. She wished they had never come to Town. She had been happy at home in Leicestershire, and she would have been quite content to marry Mr. Collier and dedicate her life to assisting him in his work, with no trace of regret for what might have been.

But now. . . now she found herself obsessed with a man who was everything the vicar was not, everything she should most despise. Lord Mannerly was rude, arrogant, and self-centered, and always gave one the uncomfortable feeling that he was mocking one. Furthermore, he cared nothing for propriety, or he would not pay the most marked attentions to a young lady who was already promised to another.

Here her frown deepened. Olivia would have been happy in Leicestershire, too, and she and Harry would have been married just as everyone had always expected. But what woman would prefer Harry's attentions to those of the marquess of Mannerly? Perhaps strangest of all was the vague suspicion that, were Olivia to change her mind and marry Lord Mannerly instead, the loss would be her own as much as her brother's.

Finding no answers either in holy writ or in the raindrops chasing one another down the window pane, she rose to go in search of her embroidery. She was not generally fond of needlework, but at present she had need of some activity—*any* activity—to distract her mind from thoughts she would prefer not to dwell on. She was just crossing the entrance hall when the door knocker sounded. Coombes hurried to answer it, and a moment later Lord Mannerly entered the house, just as if her thoughts had somehow summoned him. His many-caped greatcoat dripped water, as did his curly-brimmed beaver, and with these additions to an already imposing frame, he seemed to Georgina to fill the entire room. The effect was only slightly diminished when Coombes swept the wet articles from his lordship's person and bore them away, leaving Georgina to usher her noble guest into the parlor.

"D-Do come in, my lord," she said, suddenly short of breath. "What brings you out in this weather?"

"Surely three charming ladies under one roof are sufficient to tempt any man to brave the elements, Miss Hawthorne," he riposted, bowing over her hand.

"Three? Oh, yes, of course, three," she amended quickly,

remembering her brother's disguise.

"Tell me, how does your grandmother fare this morning?"

"She—she is indisposed, sir."

Mannerly nodded. "I thought perhaps she might be."

"I—I will tell her you called, my lord."

"But may I not see her and offer her my best wishes for a quick recovery?" protested the marquess.

"She—she is quite ill, sir," answered Georgina, casting a nervous glance toward the staircase leading to the bedchambers above. "She is not receiving visitors."

"I daresay she has the headache," suggested Mannerly, watching her through narrowed eyes.

"I—I believe she does."

"And Miss Darby? Is she, too, ill?"

Georgina looked visibly relieved. "I believe she is merely fatigued from last night's visit to Vauxhall Gardens."

"Quite likely. I understand she had a very busy evening."

It seemed to Georgina as if Lord Mannerly were speaking in riddles, but to what purpose, she could not begin to guess. "I am sure we all had a busy evening, my lord. There is so much to see and do at Vauxhall."

"While I have seen the gardens too many times to find them a novelty, I must confess that I, for one, was certainly never bored," agreed the marquess.

Nor was he so utterly lost to propriety as Georgina supposed, for he was fully aware of the awkwardness attending a young lady entertaining a gentleman without a chaperone present. He therefore took his leave without further ado, promising to give himself the pleasure of calling again at a later date, at which time he hoped he would find Lady Hawthorne and Miss Darby in better health. Having received his still-damp outer garments from Coombes, he waved the butler away, professing himself capable of showing himself out. But his capability in this regard was perhaps overstated, for as he drew the door closed, it met the frame with a slam that seemed to shake the entire house. Immediately it flew open again to reveal the marquess, all repentance.

"I beg your pardon," he said, casting upon Georgina a look of wide-eyed innocence which sat ill upon his saturnine countenance. "It must have been the wind."

Then he shut the door once again, more gently this time, and hailed a passing hackney, smiling to himself as he pictured Sir Harry somewhere upstairs, clutching his throbbing head.

☙

While Georgina perused the Good Book, Olivia remained cloistered in her bedchamber. Sitting in the window seat, she relived in vivid detail the disastrous events of the previous weeks as she stared morosely at the leaden skies. When she recalled her naïveté in thinking she could win Harry's affections by encouraging Lord Mannerly's attentions, she knew not whether to laugh or cry. She pressed her knuckles to her bruised lips, recalling Harry's kiss. She had waited all her life for Harry to take her into his arms, and when the long-awaited event had finally come to pass, it had been all wrong. Certainly it was not love that had inspired his actions, but fury. Then she had committed her crowning folly in slapping his face, which surely must have killed forever any affection he might once have felt for her. She should have been content to make a loveless match, and trust to Time to earn her a place in Harry's heart.

Upon hearing the sharp rap of the knocker on the front door below, she leaped up to peer at the front stoop, her heart pounding at the prospect of seeing Harry there. But alas, the great-coated figure standing in the rain was clearly too tall to be Sir Harry, and this assessment was confirmed a moment later, when the door was opened and Lord Mannerly's well-modulated tones reached her ears.

She sank back down to the window seat, unwilling to face the marquess's mocking eyes and knowing smile. For this part was harder to bear than all the rest. She had slapped poor Harry, only to discover not five minutes later that he had been right all along in his estimation of Lord Mannerly's character. When she thought of the liberties he had taken with her—no, that she had allowed him to take!—her face burned hot with shame. Surely Harry would despise her if he knew! How ironic it would be if, by conspiring to win him, she only succeeded in giving him a disgust of her instead! As she idly traced a raindrop's progress down her window pane, she thought longingly of her fiancé and wondered where he was and what he was doing, little supposing that at that moment Sir Harry was ensconced in the bedchamber two doors down, nursing a very sore head.

❧

It was a haggard-looking "Lady Hawthorne" who, thanks to numerous pots of strong coffee and more than a few dunkings of his head into a bowl of cold water, made his way downstairs that evening dressed in full ball regalia of puce satin evening gown, long kid gloves, and an elaborately coifed wig topped by a crimson turban with a single purple ostrich plume curving artistically over his left temple. His aching head notwithstanding, it was Wednesday night, and to fail to appear at Almack's Assembly Rooms would be to invite unwelcome speculation. Olivia was still in her room, but Georgina was already waiting below, demurely attired in a gown of pale green which complemented her copper curls to perfection. When Olivia finally appeared, not even Sir Harry could say with honesty that his love was enjoying her customary good looks. To be sure, her coiffure was flawless and her gown unexceptionable, but the pink satin which should have brought out the roses in her cheeks only called attention to their absence, and the rouge with which her maid had attempted to correct this deficiency merely served to emphasize the pallor beneath.

"You are looking well, Olivia," said Georgina perhaps a bit too brightly.

"Thank you, Georgina," Olivia said without conviction, then turned to address the older woman. "Good evening, Lady Hawthorne. I trust you are quite recovered."

"Yes, quite." Sir Harry stepped forward to take her hands in his, wincing only slightly as the hall clock loudly chimed the hour. "And you, Miss Darby?"

"Very well, thank you."

There seemed very little to say after that, and it was a subdued trio indeed that ascended into the carriage and set out for King Street.

The rain had ceased by early evening, and all of those fortunate enough to have vouchers seemed to have leaped at the opportunity to get out after a day spent indoors. The Assembly Rooms were even more crowded than usual, and the lemonade was even weaker, as if watered down to accommodate the greater numbers. The closeness of the rooms, combined with the stifling humidity, produced an oppressive heat; the Hawthorne party found seats along the wall and quickly sought recourse to their fans.

Georgina, with the natural ebullience of youth, seemed the least affected by the heat. Since her waltz with Lord Mannerly at Vauxhall Gardens, word had quickly spread among the young bucks of the *ton* that Miss Hawthorne did waltz, and that divinely. She found herself sought after with an enthusiasm that recalled her days as the belle of Leicestershire, and discovered that her innocent enjoyment of her popularity was, perhaps, not so sinful after all, when compared to her more dangerous fascination with the marquess of Mannerly.

When the clock chimed the dreaded hour of eleven with no sign of Sir Harry, Olivia found that the oppressive heat matched the oppression of her spirits. She did stand up when solicited, although with such a lack of interest that her would-be partners soon sought the company of more willing ladies. Far from being offended, Olivia was content to sit beside her chaperone, searching the crush in the forlorn hope that Sir Harry had somehow slipped in without her having seen him, and might at any moment separate himself from the crowd and come in search of her.

When it became increasingly obvious that this joyous event would not take place, she sank even deeper into the dismals. Why should Harry beg to dance with the fiancée who had struck him in anger only twenty-four hours earlier? Or did he still consider her his fiancée at all? Perhaps he would wish to cry off. At this point, logic overcame melancholy. Sir Harry was too much the gentleman to do anything so shabby but, perhaps worse, he might *wish* he could. Olivia knew she should set him free rather than trap him in a marriage he no longer wanted, but doubted she possessed the strength to follow a course of action so opposed to her own desires.

As the night progressed, the ladies' faces grew shinier and the gentlemen's cravats wilted. Georgina's latest partner, a ruddy-faced young gentleman whose once-magnificent shirtpoints now sagged against his neck, mopped his face with his handkerchief while Georgina, her red hair curling riotously from the heat, excused herself to the powder room for the same purpose. Olivia plied her fan with renewed vigor, then, turning to make some idle remark to her chaperone, noticed Lady Hawthorne's hands trembling.

"Are you much bothered by the heat, my lady?" she asked. "Shall I fetch you some lemonade?"

Sir Harry, who under normal circumstances would have spurned such an insipid drink, was in no condition to refuse. "If you please," he rasped.

Olivia did not hesitate. She made her way to the refreshment room as quickly as possible, given the crowds, and at last returned bearing a glass of the pale liquid, *sans* ice.

"It is not very cool, I'm afraid," she said by way of apology, offering this dubious refreshment to the dowager.

"Quite all right," said the *faux* Lady Hawthorne, accepting the offering and raising it gratefully to her lips. As her head tilted upwards,

Olivia noticed that the jaunty ostrich plume which had curled over Lady Hawthorne's left temple now drooped against her ear. The heavy powder and rouge favored by so many of Lady Hawthorne's generation had long since melted away, revealing the dowager's bare cheek—which bore the unmistakable imprint of a lady's hand.

If Olivia had still been holding the glass of lemonade, it surely would have slipped from her nerveless fingers and crashed to the floor. Her chaperone, Lady Hawthorne, and her fiancé, Sir Harry Hawthorne, whom she had slapped at Vauxhall Gardens a scant twenty-four hours earlier, were one and the same.

Olivia stared at the beloved, familiar features beneath the curled and powdered wig. How could she not have seen it? Of course, she had never actually met the real Lady Hawthorne, although a very fine Romney portrait over the fireplace in the drawing room at Hawthorne Grange revealed a tall, mannish woman with a marked resemblance to Harry, who did look quite different without his sidewhiskers. Still, she of all people, who had loved him from her earliest childhood, should have recognized him through any disguise.

"I beg your pardon, Miss Darby," Lord Mannerly's voice, smooth as satin, cut through her thoughts, "but I believe the next dance is mine."

She blinked at the marquess like one awakening from a particularly vivid dream. At that moment she could have cheerfully wished him to the devil, along with all the swirling, sweating dancers and the musicians whose strident fiddles grated painfully on her taut nerves. But one dared not make a scene at Almack's, so there was nothing Olivia could do but place her hand on his proffered arm and, with one last helpless glance at Sir Harry, allow the marquess to lead her into the set.

The movements of the dance prevented conversation, for which Olivia was profoundly thankful. Still, the intricate figures were not sufficient to occupy her mind. What had possessed Harry to attempt such a masquerade, and had he any notion of the risk he was running? Did he not realize that if he were discovered, the ensuing scandal would mean ruin? Powerless to demand answers of Sir Harry, she could only watch him helplessly as the questions spun around and around in her brain, faster and faster, turning in upon one another in a dance more convoluted than the cotillion ever was.

Her frequent, furtive glances at her duenna were not lost on her partner. "Something has happened to distress you, Miss Darby," Lord Mannerly observed, when the figures of the dance brought them back together. "What is it, if I may be so bold?"

Olivia shook her head. "'Tis nothing, my lord, I assure you."

"Are you quite certain? You look a bit pale."

"How very ungentlemanly of you to say so," replied Olivia, forcing a smile. "Since you will have it, I confess I feel a bit faint, but I daresay it is only the heat. It will soon pass, I am sure."

"Perhaps, but you will no doubt feel better for a bit of privacy."

Brooking no argument, he took her elbow and led her from the floor. Their departure in the middle of a dance, which would have raised eyebrows under normal circumstances, was on this occasion scarcely remarked at all, several other ladies of delicate constitution having already succumbed to the heat and made similar exits. Having reached a small antechamber along the wall, Lord Mannerly drew back the heavy curtain and ushered Olivia within. After seating her on a chair, he took the fan which hung from a satin cord about her wrist and began to waft it gently to and fro.

"Thank you, my lord," she said with a grateful sigh. "I feel better already. If you will bring Lady Hawthorne to me, I would be much obliged."

"I am, of course, yours to command, but I am reluctant to leave you alone, my dear," said the marquess smoothly, regarding Olivia through narrowed eyes. "I am sure it must be most distressing to learn that one's affianced husband has been capering about London in the guise of a woman."

# 11

The devil is a gentleman.
PERCY BYSSHE SHELLEY, *Peter Bell the Third*

Olivia's abrupt departure with Lord Mannerly had not gone unnoticed by Sir Harry. Indeed, as he watched the marquess sweep Olivia into the secluded alcove, his eyebrows drew together in a frown, and his mouth assumed a hard, taut line. Claiming his prerogative as both her chaperone and her affianced bridegroom, he rose from his chair and made his way toward the antechamber as quickly as was possible in the evening slippers which pinched his toes quite painfully.

He was perhaps halfway to his goal when he heard himself (or rather, his grandmother) hailed with some urgency. Turning, he beheld a breathless Colonel Gubbins bearing down upon him, his corsets creaking with every step.

"My dear Lady Hawthorne," panted this worthy, mopping his brow with a large and decidedly damp handkerchief. "How delightful to see you here!"

"Likewise, I'm sure," replied his object, retreating before the gallant's advance. "Now, if you will please excuse me—"

"Oh, cruel!" cried the Colonel, drawing the dowager's gloved hand through the crook of his arm. "Can you not spare one moment for an old friend?"

Sir Harry would have hastened his retreat, but found it prevented by the colonel's grip on his hand. "I am very busy, Colonel. My charges, you know—"

"Are they such hurly-burly females that you must watch them every minute? I'll not believe such a thing, not with you, my lady, for their example!"

"You are too kind—"

"And you, alas, are unkindness itself! But mere maidenly modesty will not—cannot!—deter me. My feelings are too powerful. I must persevere!"

In a tactical maneuver which Lord Mannerly might have envied, the military man steered the hapless Sir Harry into a nearby antechamber. There, to his dismay, he found his hand released, but only so that the colonel might take his inamorata into his arms.

"But say you will be mine, and I will be a happy man!" declared the colonel.

"Colonel Gubbins, I must insist—!" cried Sir Harry in real alarm, struggling to free himself.

"Don't try to fight it, my dear. This is bigger than the both of us!"

"Colonel, please!"

But his protests fell on deaf ears. Puckering his lips and squeezing his eyes shut, Colonel Gubbins leaned forward with every intention of stealing a kiss from his lady fair. In the nick of time, Sir Harry remembered the heavy brass paperweight he had carried in his reticule ever since his brush with London's criminal element.

"Forgive me, Colonel, for what I am about to do," said Sir Harry.

And with a strength born of desperation, he wrested free of the larger man's grasp and, swinging his reticule by its silken cords, landed a blow to the colonel's ear.

"There!" pronounced Sir Harry with no small satisfaction, as the stunned colonel staggered back against the wall, clutching his injured auricle. "Perhaps that will teach you not to force unwelcome advances onto a lady!"

And sweeping the curtain aside, he quitted the chamber with great dignity.

☙

Olivia's eyes opened wide. Suddenly, in spite of the stifling heat, she felt chilled. "I—I beg your pardon?"

"But I am speaking of Sir Harry, of course. Tell me, Miss Darby, when did you learn his secret? I confess my suspicions were aroused that night at Covent Garden, but I did not discover the whole truth until last night, when I watched your enterprising bridegroom enter his town house through an upper-story window."

Olivia rose with a jerk. "I—I haven't the faintest idea what you are talking about, my lord."

"Oh, but I think you do."

"Nonsense! Why would anyone pull such a preposterous stunt?"

"Perhaps for love of a lady?" suggested the marquess. "A lady whom he was afraid of losing to another?"

In spite of her predicament, something akin to joy pierced the veil of Olivia's fear and misery. If Harry had taken such a foolish risk for her sake, he must love her more than she had ever dreamed possible. If only it were not too late! For his sake, and for the sake of their future, she must keep a cool head.

"I think you are being most unkind to poor Lady Hawthorne," she informed the marquess with surprising calm. "I will own, she looks somewhat hag-ridden tonight, but she became quite ill last night at Vauxhall."

Lord Mannerly remained unmoved. "Sir Harry is certainly ill, Miss Darby, but I can assure you the damage was done at White's, not Vauxhall—as any number of gentlemen can attest, should you be so indiscreet as to make inquiries."

Having failed to convince the marquess with one argument, Olivia tried another. "Tell me, my lord, if you are so convinced that I am aware of this—this so-called charade, why do you find it necessary to bring it to my attention?"

"All in good time, my dear. Your obvious distress suggests that you are aware of the consequences Sir Harry will face should the *ton* learn of his folly. He would, of course, be ruined, to say nothing of the damage to your own reputation if it should become known that you are residing under the same roof. Miss Hawthorne, pious though she undoubtedly is, could hardly be considered an adequate chaperone."

In spite of her fears, Olivia's chin rose, and she looked the marquess squarely in the eye. "Am I to understand, sir, that you intend to make Harry's—indiscretions—public?"

The look Mannerly gave her was one of wounded innocence. "You misjudge me, my dear. I only seek to offer you the opportunity to, shall we say, safeguard Sir Harry's interests."

"If blackmail is your intention, my lord, you must know that you already possess more wealth than Harry or I could ever hope to give you!"

"No, no! Nothing so crass, my dear. I simply offer you an exchange: my silence for your virtue."

"*What*?" cried Olivia, aghast.

"Ah, we begin to understand one another. Good! The whole thing is quite simple, really. One brief assignation, after which you will be free to return to your own home, where you may marry your baronet before anyone, including Sir Harry, is the wiser. As for myself, I will consider the matter forgotten."

"But—but this is monstrous!"

"Monstrous? Spare me the Cheltenham tragedies, I beg you! You might even find it quite enjoyable. At any rate, 'tis Hobson's choice for you, my dear. If you are to preserve your reputation, you must sacrifice your virtue. Ironic, is it not? Naturally, I understand such a momentous decision cannot be made on impulse. I will give you until tomorrow afternoon to consider. Then we shall meet at Kensington Gardens at, say, three o'clock. There you may give me your answer."

Without awaiting a reply (which Olivia could not have uttered, at any rate), Mannerly strode to the curtain and grasped its velvet folds, then paused and turned back.

"By the bye, I should not mention any of this to Sir Harry, if I were you. Things might be the worse for him if you do."

Then he was gone. Sunk in despair, Olivia collapsed onto her chair and buried her face in her hands. And it was here, a short time later, that Sir Harry found her.

"Miss Darby?" He peered through the curtains and, seeing Olivia's grief-stricken countenance, momentarily forgot his alter ego. Crossing the small chamber in two strides, he dropped to one knee before her chair and seized her by the shoulders. "Livvy! Whatever is the matter?"

His unconscious use of the childhood nickname almost proved more than Olivia could bear, but remembering Lord Mannerly's parting shot, she pulled herself together with an effort. "'Tis nothing but a foolish megrim, Har—my lady," she assured him. "But, pray, would you mind very much taking me home?"

"Of course not!" he said, giving her a measured look which she knew not quite how to interpret. "Only wait here while I find Georgina."

If the trio which set had out from Curzon Street earlier that evening had been subdued, the one that returned was positively morose. Even Georgina had succumbed to the combination of stifling heat and vigorous exercise, her low spirits exacerbated, no doubt, by the disappointing behavior of Lord Mannerly, who had arrived at Almack's just before eleven, danced a single dance with Olivia, and quitted the Assembly Rooms almost immediately upon escorting her from the floor. Although she bore her future sister-in-law no ill will, she would have thought Olivia would agree that one admirer per lady was a suitably even distribution.

As Georgina mounted the stairs to her bedchamber, Olivia would have followed, had not Sir Harry laid his gloved hand on her arm to detain her.

"Yes?" she asked, looking beyond the female garb and powdered wig to the man she knew lurked beneath. "What is it?"

Sir Harry stroked his jaw in a gesture so achingly familiar that, had she not already guessed his secret, surely would have given him away. "My dear, if you are in some sort of trouble, had you best not tell Harry? He—he is—quite fond of you, you know."

*I should not mention any of this to Sir Harry. . . Things might be the worse for him, if you do. . . .* Lord Mannerly's parting words hung between them like a tangible presence.

"No," said Olivia, shaking her head. "'Tis nothing. Good night, Lady Hawthorne." She began to turn away, then on sudden impulse, turned back and kissed Harry's painted cheek.

Fighting the urge to take her in his arms, Sir Harry watched in silence as she climbed the stairs. "Fond," he muttered contemptuously after she had disappeared from view at the top of the landing. What an inane, insipid, totally inadequate word! He was fond of riding, hunting, and whist; he was not, nor had he ever been, fond of Olivia Darby. He was in love with her, passionately and desperately in love, and he chafed under the knowledge that he, trapped in the charade he had begun with the best of intentions, was powerless to help her in her distress.

That it had something to do with Lord Mannerly, he was certain. He was sensitive now to Olivia's moods in a way he had never been before, and although she had seemed somewhat melancholy earlier in the evening, she had certainly not been distraught until her *tête-à-tête* with

Mannerly. Sir Harry's mouth took on a grim aspect. He had known from the first that Mannerly would be trouble.

As he mounted the stairs in Olivia's wake, a plan began to form in his mind. If she would not confide in "Lady Hawthorne," perhaps he could prevail upon her to confide in Sir Harry. He would send "Lady Hawthorne" out tomorrow on some pretext, then return to his Stratton Street lodgings for a change of clothes before paying a formal call in Curzon Street. Lastly, he would profess his undying love for Olivia, and beg her to grant him the opportunity to prove it. And if that proof should call for running Mannerly through with a sword or putting a bullet through his brain at Paddington Green, so much the better. He had been spoiling for the opportunity ever since that first night at Almack's when he had seen his Livvy in the marquess's arms.

Feeling more cheerful already, he took off the offending slippers and strode boldly to his room to give instructions to Higgins.

# 12

Necessity never made a good bargain.
BENJAMIN FRANKLIN, *Poor Richard's Almanac*

Olivia did not rise from her bed before noon, having passed a restless night disturbed by troubling dreams—when, indeed, she was able to sleep at all. When at last she arrived at the breakfast table, she was met with the information that Lady Hawthorne had gone out on a shopping expedition. For this Olivia was grateful; she feared she lacked the strength to be all day in Sir Harry's company without breaking down and confessing the whole, to his everlasting downfall.

The cheery breakfast room, decorated in sunny shades of yellow and white, seemed to mock Olivia's despair. She poured herself a cup of chocolate and took a seat at the table, where she toyed with a slice of toast and made a desultory attempt at conversation with her future sister-in-law. Georgina, too, was unusually reticent and continued so even after breakfast, seemingly preoccupied with her needlework and her own thoughts. On any other occasion, this might have evoked comment, but on this particular day, Olivia's mind was too taken up with her own dilemma to notice the megrims of another.

What had she done to poor Harry, and whatever was she to do now? If only she had listened when he had warned her to have nothing to do with Mannerly! To be sure, it was Harry who would suffer the most if he were exposed. Olivia cared little for her own reputation, for if their unseemly living arrangements were to be discovered, the only result for her would be a hasty marriage and a discreet removal to the country—precisely what she had wished for all along. But how could she subject Harry to the scorn of the very society in which he thrived? Such a course of action was too contemptible to contemplate.

On the other hand, if she submitted to Lord Mannerly's nefarious scheme, it would be tantamount to planting cuckold's horns on Harry's head before he had even reached the altar. It was even possible that, some nine months after the "brief assignation" of which the marquess spoke, she might present Harry with an heir who was not even his child, but Mannerly's. Every feeling revolted at such an act of betrayal! But could she in all honor do less, to protect him from utter ruin?

The early post brought some slight distraction in the form of a letter from Mrs. Darby. Olivia's hopes soared. Lord Mannerly had "suggested" that she not tell Harry of his intentions, but he had said nothing about not telling her mama. Eagerly she broke the seal and scanned the crossed and re-crossed lines. Liza and her son were both doing well, it seemed, and George, her husband, was expected to return within the week. Barring any complications, Mrs. Darby hoped to rejoin her daughter in London by Tuesday next. She trusted her daughter and Georgina were enjoying their Season, and could not sufficiently express her gratitude to Lady Hawthorne for taking the girls under her wing.

Olivia's hopes plummeted once more. Her mama would be devastated if she discovered she had left her daughter to the chaperonage of none other than her intended bridegroom, and Olivia was not at all certain she could depend upon her mother to keep her distress suitably private. No, she had best not write to her mama. But, she thought, perhaps there was another to whom she could turn for assistance.

Hurrying to the drawing room, she seated herself at an elegant rosewood writing table and, after locating vellum and a quill, began to write:

*My dear Lady Hawthorne, I beg you will forgive my impertinence in writing to you, but I feel it my duty to inform you that your grandson and my fiancé, Sir Harry Hawthorne, has fallen into difficulties from which you alone would seem to have the power to extricate him. . . .*

Olivia's quill fairly flew across the page, as the whole story of her foolish whim, Sir Harry's masquerade, and her current dilemma came pouring out. When she had finished, she sealed the letter and summoned a footman.

"Charles, see that this is delivered to Lady Hawthorne—that is, Lady Hawthorne's *lodgings* in Laura Place, Bath. The messenger is to ride all night, if necessary, but this letter must be delivered without delay."

"Yes, miss." Having received the sealed missive, Charles shifted his weight uneasily from one foot to the other. "Er, begging your pardon, miss, but won't Lady Hawthorne's lodgings be empty, her ladyship being in Town?"

"Nonsense! Lady Hawthorne employs a—a companion, who remains in residence there," replied Olivia, improvising rapidly. "Now, be on your way, and quickly!"

The footman set out on his errand, and Olivia let out a long breath. The letter was on its way. If only it might reach its destination before it was too late!

One by one the minutes slipped slowly by, until the time came for Olivia to meet Lord Mannerly and give him the answer that would determine Sir Harry's fate. She allowed her maid to outfit her in a gray walking dress of no particular style or beauty, so as not to call undue attention to herself, and had just finished tying the strings of her bonnet when the door knocker sounded. A moment later Sir Harry stood before her, every inch the Town beau in a blue coat of Bath superfine, pantaloons of a delicate yellow hue, and gleaming Hessian boots. To Olivia, the very sight of him was like a knife in her bosom. How could she give herself to Lord Mannerly when her heart belonged only to Harry? And yet, how could she save her virtue at his expense?

"Why, Harry, what a pleasant surprise," said Olivia with a pathetic attempt at a smile. "What brings you here?"

"What better reason than to see you?" Sir Harry replied gallantly, taking her gloved hands in his.

If he had harbored any doubts about Olivia's mental state, her appearance would have certainly put them to rest. Her fine eyes held a hunted look, and seemed overly large in her pale and drawn face. Dark half-circles underneath testified to a sleepless night. Sir Harry, far from being repulsed by her haggard appearance, found all his protective instincts fully aroused.

"But I am fortunate not to have missed you," he continued, wisely keeping these unflattering observations to himself. "Are you going out?"

Olivia darted a furtive glance at the clock. It would never do to be late; Lord Mannerly might think she was not coming. "Indeed, I am, as you can see."

She tried to draw her hands from Sir Harry's grasp, but his fingers only tightened over hers. "Can it not wait? There is something particular I must tell you—"

"I—I'm afraid it can't."

"In that case, dismiss your maid, and I shall escort you," persisted Sir Harry.

"I should not wish to impose—"

"'Tis no imposition, I assure you."

"I—I am only going shopping for gloves and stockings and the like," fudged Olivia. "You would be shockingly bored."

"Believe me, Livvy, I could never be bored in your company."

Olivia cast another glance at the clock. She would have to hurry to make her rendezvous in time. How long would Mannerly wait before working his mischief?

"For heaven's sake, Harry," she cried in desperation, "for my first month in London, you seemed to have forgotten my existence, and now you wish to shadow my every move! Can you not see that I prefer to be alone?"

Pain flared ever so briefly in Sir Harry's eyes before his face became a mask, devoid of all emotion. "You have made that abundantly plain," he said with crushing formality. "And so I bid you good day, madam."

Olivia could only watch miserably as Sir Harry turned without another word and quitted the house. Unfortunately, she had not the luxury of repining for what might have been, for the hands of the large hall clock inched ever closer to three, and she dared not keep Lord Mannerly waiting.

"Come, Mary," she said to her servant, and mistress and maid left the house in Sir Harry's wake.

They had progressed some way down the street when a fashionably clad figure emerged from the corner whence he had once scaled the wall to the window. Something havey-cavey was going on, and Sir Harry Hawthorne intended to find out what it was. He waited until Olivia was some distance ahead, then fell into step behind her.

ꟹ

So quick were Olivia's steps that both she and her maid were out of breath by the time they reached their destination. Once the royal playground of the Hanovers, Kensington Gardens had been opened to the public in the last century, but the absence of the Court had eventually robbed the Gardens of their appeal. The *beau monde* rarely frequented Kensington anymore, and Olivia assumed this was precisely the reason the marquess had selected it as a rendezvous. She recalled that Princess Lieven had gone so far as to say that good society no longer visited the Gardens except to drown itself. If these unfortunates had found themselves in circumstances half so dire as her own, reflected Olivia, gazing at the Long Water which separated the Gardens from the more fashionable Hyde Park, she could easily see the appeal.

Instructing her maid to wait for her, she set out down one of the grassed walks in the direction of the Round Pond, which she judged to be a likely meeting place. In this assessment she was correct, for it was here that, a short time later, Lord Mannerly joined her.

"Ah, Miss Darby," he said, bowing over her hand. "I had quite given you up."

"I was—delayed," she offered by way of explanation, remembering the pain in Harry's eyes at her curt dismissal.

The marquess drew her hand through his arm, and they set out together along the grassy walk. When he spoke again, it was as offhand as if he were discussing something of no more importance than the weather. "And have you considered my offer, Miss Darby?"

Olivia stared fixedly ahead, avoiding her companion's gaze. "I have."

"And what decision have you reached?"

She took a deep breath. "I have elected to accept your terms, my lord."

"A wise decision, my dear, and one which I am sure you will not regret."

Olivia could not let this comment pass unchallenged. "I fear I cannot share your confidence, sir, but since you give me no choice—"

The marquess's eyebrows rose in mock surprise. "No choice? My dear, you wound me to the quick! Did I not offer you *two* alternatives from which to choose?"

"You did," conceded Olivia, transferring her gaze to her kid half-boots.

"And did you not select the one you found preferable?"

Her reply was little more than a whisper. "Yes."

"Good! For a moment there you alarmed me. Now that that is settled, we have only to work out the particulars. There is to be a masquerade at Vauxhall Gardens on Monday night. Meet me at the pavilion at midnight, and wear a white domino. We shall conduct our business, and then I shall return you to your party before you are missed."

"I haven't a white domino," put in Olivia, not without satisfaction.

Having come so close to the achievement of his ambition, Lord Mannerly was not about to surrender over a mere matter of dress. "I shall consider it an honor to provide you with one," he replied.

"I have heard that masquerades are not at all the thing," persisted Olivia. "What if—my duenna—will not allow me to attend?"

"Come, come, my dear," chided the marquess. "You must know that Sir Harry will deny you nothing. I am sure you will be able to bring him around."

"And if I cannot?"

Mannerly shrugged. "If I find myself alone at midnight with nothing to occupy me, who knows what mischief I might find with which to busy myself? Idle hands, as Miss Hawthorne might say, are the devil's workshop, you know."

Olivia nodded, recognizing the threat in the seemingly innocuous quotation. "I—I shall be there."

"Until Monday, then," said the marquess. Taking her hand in his, he turned it over and pressed a kiss into her palm.

She made no farewells, but summoned her maid and quickly departed, too shaken to notice the fashionable young man loitering near the gates behind a concealing hedge.

But he saw her, and it took every ounce of strength he possessed not to call out to her. For Sir Harry, it seemed, had just been dealt a terrible blow. Olivia—his Livvy, whom he loved more than life, was seeing Lord Mannerly on the sly! He would not have credited it had he not seen it himself, the way Mannerly kissed her hand, the way Olivia looked demurely away, too overcome to meet her lover's eye.

He thought of her as she had appeared that morning, with her pale face and her hollow eyes. It had been he, not Mannerly, who had put that look there. Good God! Did she find the prospect of marriage to him so intolerable? Had she been pressured to accept his suit? No, he could not credit it. Something had happened since her arrival in London to make her change her mind. And he knew, all too well, what that something was. He knew, because it had happened to him, too. Olivia had fallen in love.

It was his own fault; that was the worst of it. He'd had more than twenty years to fix his interest with her, twenty years to win her love, but he hadn't even bothered to make the attempt. Small wonder, then, that she had succumbed so easily to Lord Mannerly's practiced lovemaking.

Of course, an honorable man would let her go. An honorable man would release her so that she might marry according to the dictates of her heart. And if it were some other man—*any* other man—he would do it, no matter how much it tore him apart. Unfortunately, he had only to think of his Livvy lying in Mannerly's arms to realize just how dishonorable he could be.

Sunk in despondence, he returned to his Stratton Street lodgings to resume his disguise, and found his valet in a rare taking.

"Oh, sir, it is too dreadful to be borne," fretted Higgins, wringing his hands.

"Good Lord, what is it now?" groaned Sir Harry, tossing his hat and gloves onto a small side table.

"I'm afraid I've been found out, sir," Higgins confessed as he helped his master out of his coat. "The talk belowstairs is that you—Lady Hawthorne, that is—are keeping a lover in your, er, her pocket by dressing him—that would be myself, sir—as a woman."

Having delivered himself of this alarming disclosure, Higgins braced himself for the expected storm, but to his amazement, Sir Harry's lips twitched. Then his master chuckled, and finally laughed out loud.

"My grandmother, keeping a lover?" he said when his mirth had subsided sufficiently to permit coherent speech. "And you're supposed to be the man? Thank you, Higgins, you'll never know how badly I needed a laugh just now. Poor fellow! Have they been giving you a difficult time of it?"

"No one has accused me in so many words, sir, although the veiled hints of the footmen can be a bit difficult to take at times."

"Well, rub along as best you can for now. It should not be long before Mrs. Darby returns, and then I shall send 'Lady Hawthorne' back to Bath, where she belongs. Then, I promise, your sufferings will not go unrewarded."

"I know, I know," said the valet with a sigh. "On the day you wed Miss Darby, my wages will be doubled."

Sir Harry's laughter died, and the amusement which had lit his eyes a moment earlier gave way to a bleakness that the servant could not recall seeing there before. "As to that, Higgins, I shouldn't count my money just yet if I were you."

After leaving Kensington Gardens, Lord Mannerly charted a direct course for the business establishment of one Madame Franchot, a fashionable modiste from whom he had occasionally purchased gifts of an intimate nature for the various barques of frailty who had enjoyed his protection over the years. Madame Franchot (who in spite of her Continental surname originally hailed from Manchester) was delighted to see the marquess, for his tastes were always unerring and usually expensive. Upon discovering that his lordship required a domino, Madame produced for his inspection a bolt of her best black satin.

"Here I have just the thing," pronounced the modiste. "Look, if you will, at the quality of the weave. Cheaper satins may be found, but none with this texture. Is it not exquisite, milord?"

"Yes, yes, very nice, but the color is all wrong," said milord, dismissing Madame Franchot's finest stock with a wave. "Have you anything in white?"

"A white domino? How beautiful, and how unique! She will break hearts, yes?"

"Only one," replied the marquess with a mysterious smile.

Madame Franchot submitted a second bolt for his approval and, this finding favor, asked her noble patron for the lady's measurements. Mannerly conjured up a mental image of Miss Darby's trim figure and offered an estimate, the accuracy of which would have mortified Olivia and enraged Sir Harry. He then requested writing paper and a quill pen, and scrawled a short note which he desired to be delivered along with the domino as quickly as possible to Miss Darby at 27 Curzon Street. The bill, he added as an afterthought, might be sent to his Park Lane address.

Having finished his business, Lord Mannerly turned his steps toward home. Everything, it seemed, was progressing nicely, and in a scant four days his revenge would be complete. He scowled at his own indifference to this knowledge. He should be delighted that the long-anticipated *dénoûement* was at hand; yet he was no more enthralled by the imminent consummation of his scheme than he would be at the conclusion of any protracted yet necessary business transaction.

Certainly, the fault did not lie with Miss Darby. The young woman was exquisite, and any man would be more than pleased to initiate her into life's sweeter mysteries; in this sentiment, he and Sir Harry Hawthorne were in complete agreement, although he doubted Sir Harry would appreciate the comparison. No, Miss Darby's physical attributes were far from repellent. He thought, instead, that it was her lack of response to his overtures which he found rather daunting. Even resistance on her part would have been preferable, as it would have given him the challenge of overcoming her scruples. But what could any man do in the face of martyrlike resignation?

Unexpectedly, Sir Harry's younger sister, the flame-haired evangelist, came to mind. Lord Mannerly's scowl became a grin. Now *that*, he thought, would be a seduction scene well worth remembering. And for a moment, Lord Mannerly, noted *bon vivant*, almost found himself envying an unknown country vicar.

# 13

Something between a hindrance and a help.
WILLIAM WORDSWORTH, *Michael*

Unmindful of the goggle-eyed maid at her heels, Olivia trudged back to Curzon Street, her mind in a state of numbness which could only be considered a blessing. It was settled. In four days, she would surrender her virtue to the marquess of Mannerly, and he in return would forget Sir Harry's ill-advised impersonation. Or would he? Perhaps Lord Mannerly would return periodically, like a bad dream, making ever-increasing demands. Perhaps she would never be free of him.

But it was best not to think of that possibility. For now, she must persuade Harry to let her attend the masquerade at Vauxhall Gardens. Indeed, it would likely require all her powers of prevarication to express eagerness at the prospect of visiting a place upon which she never wanted to set eyes again. She wished she could share Lord Mannerly's confidence in her success. *You must know that Sir Harry will deny you nothing. . . .* If only that were true, she would beg Harry to spirit her off to Gretna and marry her out of hand, so that they need never set foot in London again.

It was with a sense of relief that she entered the Curzon Street house to discover that "Lady Hawthorne" had not yet returned. Thankfully, they were promised to attend Mrs. Brandemere's intimate dinner party that night, and Olivia's social calendar was sufficiently filled to allow little time to see Sir Harry alone. For this she was grateful, as she did not trust herself to spend the next four days in his company without breaking down and confessing the whole.

As it turned out, Mrs. Brandemere's intimate dinner, had it been held in Leicestershire, would have been a major social event. No less than forty people sat down to supper, and Olivia was treated to the ludicrous spectacle of Sir Harry, resplendent in ruby-red satin and gold net, escorted to the dining room on the arm of the pompous Duke of Worrell. One might have supposed this sight to be amusing enough that Olivia could forget, at least for a short time, the unhappy event which loomed before her. On the contrary, she cast frequent glances down the table at Sir Harry, on pins and needles lest he should at any moment betray himself. Never mind that over the last few weeks he had attended innumerable functions as Lady Hawthorne without anyone, including herself, being the wiser; she found it well nigh impossible to make idle conversation through seven courses while, at the opposite end of the table, the man she loved flirted, quite literally, with disaster.

At last Mrs. Brandemere rose from the table, signaling the ladies' withdrawal, and Olivia held her breath when Sir Harry did not immediately follow. However, he made a quick recovery, and the ladies of the party repaired to the drawing room, where Olivia surprised and gratified Sir Harry by taking a seat beside him and tucking her hand through the crook of his arm in a manner that could almost be called possessive.

Alas, Sir Harry's pleasure was short-lived, for soon after the ladies were seated and the tea tray sent for, Mrs. Brandemere begged Georgina to favor the company with a song, and she, in turn, asked Olivia to accompany her. As Olivia seated herself at the pianoforte, Mrs. Brandemere took the seat she had just vacated beside Sir Harry.

"I must say, Lady Hawthorne, your charge is not enjoying her usual blooming health," observed Mrs. Brandemere under cover of the music. "Why, when I saw her Wednesday night at Almack's, the girl looked positively hag-ridden."

Sir Harry forbore to take the bait, but only through a supreme act of will. "My dear Mrs. Brandemere, in that heat, everyone looked hag-ridden—including, if I may be so bold, your Sylvia."

"Yes, well, that's as may be, but whereas my Sylvia is fully recovered, your Miss Darby still looks rather peaked. It seems the rigors of the Season have worn her quite thin."

"How true," said Sir Harry with a soulful sigh. "She is much sought after, you know, and we receive so many invitations, we cannot possibly accept them all."

"Perhaps she should remain quietly at home more often," suggested Mrs. Brandemere. "My Sylvia, now, could dance until dawn and never appear the worse for wear. Why, I daresay after she marries, her husband will be hard pressed to find her at home!"

Sir Harry nodded in agreement. "I am sure her husband will be a most fortunate man."

"Just so," said his hostess, puzzling over this seeming *non sequitur*. "Still, I am concerned about Miss Darby. It has been my observation that gentlemen shy away from delicate females. Sir Harry will want to be sure his wife can give him an heir, you know."

"Perhaps Sir Harry looks for more than fecundity in his wife," suggested Sir Harry through clenched teeth. "If he wished to acquire a brood mare, he would have tried Tattersall's."

Olivia, perhaps mercifully, was unaware of this conversation. That part of her brain which was not intent upon her performance was given over to considering how to broach the subject of the approaching masquerade. This problem, at least, was solved through the unexpected intervention of Miss Brandemere.

"I hear there is to be a masquerade at Vauxhall on Monday," she informed the assembled ladies. "Tell me, Miss Darby, do you plan to attend?"

"A masquerade!" echoed Olivia, feigning surprise. "How delightful that sounds! Please, ma'am, may we go?" She cast eager eyes upon her duenna, hoping that Sir Harry would find it awkward to refuse such a public request.

"I hear these masked frolics are not at all the thing," asserted dour Lady Greenaway, provoking in at least one of her hearers the sudden urge to throttle her. "People will do things incognito that they would never do, were their identities known."

"Oh, but it sounds so romantic and mysterious," said Miss Brandemere on a rapturous sigh. "Just like living in a Gothic novel! Do say you will join our party, Miss Darby, and Miss Hawthorne, too."

"I cannot allow it," insisted the *faux* Lady Hawthorne. "I should be failing in my duty were I to allow my charges to attend such a disreputable gathering."

"Quite right, Lady Hawthorne," murmured Mrs. Brandemere, nodding her approval. "A quiet evening at home will do much toward setting Miss Darby's ravaged looks to rights."

"On the other hand," continued Sir Harry with a tight smile, "I am sure our dear Mrs. Brandemere would not permit her lovely daughter to attend such a function if it were not quite *comme il faut*. So long as you, ma'am, act as chaperone, my girls may go to Vauxhall with my blessing."

Olivia, amazed at having achieved her objective so easily, was not quite sure whether to be sorry or glad.

ᘓ

The following afternoon, a knock was heard on the service entrance to Sir Harry's London town house. Since Cook was already well into preparations for the salmon in shrimp sauce which was to form the centerpiece for the evening meal, she commanded the scullery maid to answer the door. Obediently, young Peg left off paring potatoes to follow these new orders, knowing all the while that Cook would later scold her for not having finished the potatoes quickly enough. However, she soon decided a scold was a small price to pay, for upon opening the door, she beheld a handsome young delivery boy bearing a bandbox from a very prestigious (and very expensive) Bruton Street modiste.

"Package for Miss Darby," said the lad, favoring Peg with an appraising stare.

"I'll give it to 'er maid, I will," Peg promised, receiving the box from his hands.

"I thought maybe you was 'er," replied the young Lothario with a cocky grin.

"Pshaw! You thought I was a lady's maid?"

"Lady's maid? I thought you was Miss Darby!"

"Pshaw!" said Peg again, obviously pleased.

"Peg!" bellowed Cook. "These potatoes won't peel themselves!"

Peg closed the door on her gallant, albeit not before receiving a broad wink and a slap on her derrière, then surrendered her burden to Charles, the footman.

"Give it to Mary," she said. "It belongs to 'er mistress."

Charles dutifully carried the package up the back stairs to the family's bedchambers on the first floor, where Mary was hanging the young ladies' freshly laundered gowns back in their wardrobes. Had he stopped to consider the matter, he would have recalled that Mary currently had *two* mistresses, as she was serving both Miss Darby and Miss Hawthorne in the capacity of lady's maid. But as it was Sir Harry who paid his wages, it was not unnaturally Sir Harry's sister who came to mind. And so Charles handed the package to Mary, along with the information that it belonged to Miss Hawthorne. For her part, Mary laid it on the bed, where it waited for some time until Georgina returned to her bedchamber, at which time the lady's maid pointed it out to her.

"For me?" cried Georgina with all of a young girl's delight at being the recipient of unexpected largesse. Eagerly she untied the strings and lifted the lid. But far from solving the mystery, the contents of the bandbox merely added to it, for inside lay a domino of white silk. Raising this interesting garment for a better look, Georgina saw a piece of paper flutter to the ground. This, when she had broken the seal and read it, proved to be the most mysterious of all, for it bore a cryptic message:

*Miss D., Midnight at the pavilion. Do not fail me, or a gentleman of our acquaintance—or is it a lady?—will suffer. Yrs., etc., M.*

Georgina's eyes grew round with amazement as the significance of these words began to dawn. Why, Lord Mannerly knew about Harry, and was blackmailing Olivia! But Olivia was only the younger daughter of a colonel, and had no money of her own—at least, not when compared to Lord Mannerly's vast holdings. What, then, could he want from her? Georgina could only think of one thing, and if that were indeed what he was after, then it was no wonder Harry had taken the marquess in such dislike.

And yet, thought Georgina, stroking the silken folds of the domino, she could not believe Lord Mannerly utterly beyond redemption. Surely if someone—herself, perhaps—pointed out the error of his ways, the marquess would listen and repent. At any rate, it was clearly her Christian duty to try. But how to go about it? She could hardly broach the subject at the tea table, and at any rate, Mannerly never paid her any attention when Olivia was present.

She studied the note in her hand, as the beginnings of a plan began to form in her mind. But of course! If she wanted to see Lord Mannerly alone, she had only to be at the pavilion at midnight. No wonder Olivia had been so desperate to attend the masquerade at Vauxhall Gardens!

Quickly, she folded the domino and placed it back in the bandbox, then resealed the note with wax from her own writing table and tucked it among the white satin folds. Olivia would no doubt be expecting this package, and it would never do to let her know it had fallen into the wrong hands.

"Mary," she said, summoning her maid, "this lovely domino belongs to Miss Darby, but I have conceived such a fondness for it that I simply must have one for myself. Place an order with Madame Girot, and tell her I shall need it by Monday. Oh, and one more thing. When you return the bandbox to Miss Darby, you need not mention that it was first delivered to me."

"Yes, miss," breathed a wide-eyed Mary, bobbing a curtsy. She had not forgotten Miss Darby's rendezvous at Kensington Gardens with a man who was *not* her fiancé, and now it seemed that Miss Hawthorne was involved in some deep dealings of her own. The clandestine activities of the young ladies, when added to Lady Hawthorne's queer starts and the rumors that flew about the servant's quarters concerning her, led Mary to the inevitable conclusion that the Quality were a very strange lot. Still, where else might a plain country girl earn the exorbitant sum of twenty guineas per year? Taking the bandbox from her young mistress, she exited the room, resolving to keep her eyes open and her tongue between her teeth.

ꟹ

At precisely two o'clock on Friday afternoon in Laura Place, as Lady Hawthorne and Miss Hunnicutt were having tea, their repast was interrupted by a pounding on the door.

"See who is at the door, Mildred," said Lady Hawthorne, refilling her delicate Sèvres cup.

The long-suffering Miss Hunnicutt obediently set her own cup aside and rose to answer the door. There, to her surprise, she saw a weary and travel-stained courier and beyond him a sweating and winded horse.

"Lady Hawthorne?" panted the courier.

"No, I am her companion," said Miss Hunnicutt.

He held out a folded and sealed sheet of vellum. "Message from London, ma'am. From Miss Darby."

Miss Hunnicutt thanked him and took the missive, then instructed him to go around to the kitchen, where Cook might give him a bite to eat and, perhaps, an apple for his poor beast. Having seen him on his way, she returned to the tea table.

"A message from London, my lady," she said, delivering this epistle to the dowager. "From Miss Darby."

"Darby? Darby? Do I know anyone named Darby?"

"I believe your grandson's fiancée is a Darby, is she not?" suggested Miss Hunnicutt timidly.

"I believe you are right. Her father was a military man, if memory serves. But what can she have to say to me?"

She broke the seal and spread the single sheet. Miss Hunnicutt watched expectantly as Lady Hawthorne scanned the page, her eyebrows descending lower and lower in a frown of increasing ferocity. When at last she reached the bottom of the page, she tossed the missive onto the table and rose with an abruptness that set the tea cups clattering.

"Mildred, pack your bags at once. We must go to London."

"Oh, dear," fretted Miss Hunnicutt, tugging at her ear. "Do you think I may be losing my hearing? For a moment I thought you said—"

"At once, Mildred!" commanded Lady Hawthorne in a voice that brooked no argument. "I am going *Out*!"

# 14

If it were done when 'tis done, then 'twere well
It were done quickly.
WILLIAM SHAKESPEARE, *Macbeth*

Over the next few days, Olivia was alternately torn between dreading the approaching *dénoûement*, and wishing it might hurry so that she could do what she had to do and be done with it. Consequently, time seemed to either fly by or stand still, depending on her mood of the moment.

On Sunday, the Hawthorne party attended the morning service at the Chapel Royal, and not even the sight of the Prince Regent in attendance was enough to lift Olivia's flagging spirits. In truth, she found herself much in need of spiritual sustenance, and by a striking coincidence (or perhaps divine inspiration), the sermon text, taken from the gospel of John, might have been selected with Olivia's plight in mind.

"'Greater love hath no man," intoned the bishop, "than this: that a man lay down his life for his friend.'"

As she listened to the poignant lines, Olivia was obliged to fumble through her reticule in search of a handkerchief with which to blot her moist eyes. The bishop, seeing this response from one of his congregation, was immensely gratified, and was heard to say later that it was the first time he could recall one of his hearers having been moved to tears.

Sir Harry, seated on Olivia's right, also observed her emotional response, and was more than ever convinced that his love had gotten herself into very deep waters. In view of the scripture which had evoked such a response, he wondered just what sacrifice Olivia was being called upon to make in the name of love. He could only think of one such oblation which Lord Mannerly might desire of a young lady, and accordingly entertained distinctly unchristian thoughts toward the marquess.

Had he been less engaged in this mental exercise, he might have noticed that his younger sister, seated on his other side, was equally dewy-eyed.

At last the fateful evening arrived, and at precisely eight o'clock, Mrs. Brandemere's carriage rolled to a stop before the Curzon Street house. The coachman rapped sharply on the door knocker, and a moment later Olivia and Georgina glided across the hall toward the door, Georgina wearing her gray satin domino, Olivia in a white one which Sir Harry could not recall having seen before. He was struck with the thought that she looked somehow bridal, in spite of her pale face and haunted eyes. This melancholy reflection led him to wonder morosely just whose bride she would eventually be.

"Now, remember," he admonished, following the two young ladies as quickly as his tight slippers would allow, "stay in well-lighted areas, and keep Mrs. Brandemere in sight at all times. I begin to wish I had never given my consent to this outing. Lady Greenaway was quite right when she said they were not at all the thing."

"I promise, you will not regret it," said Olivia, her voice curiously solemn for such a festive occasion. She followed Georgina to the door, then paused and turned back, drinking in the sight of Sir Harry in his ridiculous garb as if she might never see him again.

"Olivia?" he asked, returning her gaze with a puzzled one of his own. "What is it?"

Olivia shook her head. "Nothing. Just—goodnight."

Sir Harry stood at the open door and watched until the carriage disappeared into the fog, then swung into action.

"Coombes!" he bellowed, tugging on the bell-pull with such violence that he nearly ripped it from the wall. "Hail me a hackney at once, and tell Higgins to be ready to accompany me in five minutes!"

Upon her arrival at Vauxhall, Olivia found the popular pleasure gardens strangely altered since her previous visit. To be sure, the colorful Chinese lanterns were the same, as were the wonders of the Grand Cascade and the succulent, paper-thin slices of ham available in the various supper-boxes lining the Grand Walk; the difference was in the appearance and conduct of the pleasure-seekers. Tonight the Gardens teemed with cloaked and masked figures, and the tree-lined walks rang with loud, ill-bred shrieks of laughter. A squealing shepherdess ran past with a harlequin in hot pursuit, and Olivia began to see why masquerades were frowned upon by the discerning. When a cloaked figure passed by, brushing up against Olivia in a manner that could only be deemed familiar, that affronted young lady recalled Sir Harry's parting advice, and wished that she could follow it.

Mrs. Brandemere was an exacting duenna, only allowing her charges to dance with gentlemen whom she recognized; however, after three or four cups of rack punch, her chaperonage grew noticeably more lax. Disturbing as this might have been under normal circumstances, tonight Olivia could only be grateful, as it would make it easier for her to keep her midnight assignation. However, her plans changed unexpectedly when a servant delivered a note. It was sealed with red wax, although it bore no markings which might have identified its sender. Separating herself from her chaperone, Olivia broke the seal and spread open the sheet. The message thereon was brief and to the point:

*Miss D., There has been a change in plans. Meet me at the end of the Grand Walk at midnight. Yrs., etc., M.*

Olivia read these lines with dismay, for the new point of rendezvous was considerably removed from the old, and it would take longer to reach from the supper-box where they were now situated. Glancing at her companions, Olivia found Mrs. Brandemere helping herself to yet another plate of ham, while Miss Brandemere flirted with a tall figure in a scarlet domino. Georgina had been solicited to stroll, and Olivia could see her gray-clad form taking a turn before the Rotunda on the arm of her escort, wisely remaining within view of her chaperone. Quickly, before her courage failed her, Olivia stole out of the supper-box and was soon swallowed up by the crowd milling about the Grand Walk.

Although the central part of the Gardens was overrun with masked revelers, the crowd thinned considerably once Olivia passed the pavilion. To be sure, there were still people about, but most of these seemed to be couples intent upon dalliance or, more disturbing, bucks on the prowl for unwary maidens. Several times Olivia had the distinct impression that she was being followed, but when she turned to look behind her, she saw nothing but anonymous maskers engrossed in their own pleasures, seemingly oblivious to her presence.

At last she reached her destination. Here the lights were fewer and farther between, and the trees lining the walk cast eerie shadows across her path. A Grecian temple had been erected at the end of the walk, and before this structure a tall entity in a black domino awaited. Olivia paused, waiting for Mannerly to approach her, but he showed no sign of doing so. At last, hesitantly, she closed the distance between them.

"My lord?" she asked in a voice that shook slightly.

The man in the black domino turned toward her, and that part of his face which was not hidden by a black half-mask was completely unfamiliar. "Why, no, sweeting, but I'd like to be!"

And before Olivia could protest, she found herself caught up in a smothering embrace.

"Unhand me at once, sir!" she demanded with perhaps more bravado than she felt. "I am looking for someone—"

"You've found me!" declared her gallant, punctuating this statement by pressing hot, moist lips to hers.

Olivia, stamping ineffectually at his foot with the heel of her fragile kid slipper, was unaware of the newcomer who tapped her captor on the shoulder. Not until she found herself abruptly released did she become aware of this second gentleman, also clad in a black domino, who seized the would-be Lothario by the throat, swung him around, and delivered a bruising left to the stranger's jaw.

Olivia did not linger long enough to thank her rescuer, but ran back up the Grand Walk in the direction she had come, all thoughts of her meeting with Lord Mannerly driven from her mind by fear and overwrought nerves. Upon reaching a safe distance, she looked back, wondering if perhaps it had been Lord Mannerly who had come to her rescue—how ironic *that* would have been!—but one glance informed her that this gentleman was not tall enough to be the marquess. Then, upon seeing him take two or three resolute steps in her direction, she picked up her skirts and fled.

☙

Sir Harry, having neatly disposed of Olivia's unwanted suitor, pushed back the man's hood and was disappointed to discover that the gentleman lying unconscious on the ground was not, in fact, Lord Mannerly. He should have guessed, he thought bitterly. Had it been Mannerly, would Olivia have struggled in his embrace? Suddenly he could tolerate the uncertainty no longer; he had to hear from her own lips whether or not she loved the marquess. Seeing her pause, he started in her direction, but she only hastened her retreat, and although he followed, he quickly lost sight of her in the crowd.

If Sir Harry had thought life could hold no more painful sight than that of his own Livvy fleeing from him in terror, he was soon to discover his mistake. As he approached the pavilion, the gleam of white satin caught his eye, and the scene that unfolded before him froze him in his tracks. Near the entrance to the pavilion waited a lady in white, the hood of her domino pulled forward so as to conceal her face. A tall man in a black domino approached her, raising her hand to his lips in salutation. Then, the lady nodding her assent, he drew her hand through his arm and the pair made their way toward the gates at the entrance to the garden.

Olivia's apparent submissiveness moved Sir Harry in a way that her earlier resistance had not. When he had seen her struggling in the arms of a stranger, he had been hot with fury; now he felt chilled to the very core of his being. Well, he was not going to give her up without a fight! Resolutely he pushed his way through the crowd, unmindful of the glaring looks he received from gentlemen whom he had jostled or ladies upon whose hems he had trodden.

He reached the garden entrance just in time to see a nondescript hired carriage go by at a brisk pace. Lord Mannerly's carriage, he knew, had his crest emblazoned on the panel, but whatever else Mannerly might be, he was not fool enough to attempt an elopement in a vehicle so easily recognized. Hailing a passing hackney, Sir Harry startled the driver by climbing up beside him on the box and seizing the reins from his slackened grasp.

Sir Harry was by no means a contemptible whip, and indeed might have stood some chance of overtaking his quarry, had he not been cut off by an antiquated landaulet filled with masked parvenus, all in high spirits either from the gardens' famed rack punch or from the satisfaction of a night spent among the Quality. They showed no inclination to hurry home from their night of revelry, but progressed up the Vauxhall Bridge

Road at a leisurely pace which inspired Sir Harry to air a vocabulary which had not been fully exercised since his Oxford days.

ꕤ

Olivia, meanwhile, reached the pavilion just in time to see the cloaked and masked Lord Mannerly—for surely it could be no one else—offer his arm to a lady in a white domino. No, it could not be! She could not allow Lord Mannerly to take the wrong woman, for not only would an innocent female be ruined, but the marquess would believe that she herself had intentionally arranged the switch, and poor Harry would be lost.

Unmindful of the leering glances of the masked men, she hurried toward the pavilion, but by the time she reached it, the marquess had absconded with his prey. As she stood wondering what to do next, a slight breeze stirred the shrubbery and fluttered the folds of a length of gray satin concealed therein. With a growing sense of unease, Olivia drew the length of fabric out of the greenery, and found herself holding Georgina's gray domino. Her mind recoiled in horror from the implication: Lord Mannerly had taken Georgina!

Fighting the panic which threatened to overtake her, Olivia forced herself to think rationally. She must return to Curzon Street and tell Harry, who would no doubt feel compelled to challenge Lord Mannerly to a duel. Mannerly would probably shoot him, or run him through with a sword, and all her efforts to rescue him would have led instead to his destruction.

She shook her head to clear away the unwelcome images. This was not rational thinking at all! No, what she must do was return to Mrs. Brandemere and ask to be taken home. With a firm goal to work toward, she felt much calmer, and soon located the chaperone and her daughter inside the pavilion, where Miss Brandemere was dancing with an Elizabethan courtier while her mama beamed fondly at her daughter's newest prospect.

"Mrs. Brandemere—" Olivia began.

"Just look at them, Miss Darby," said the chaperone with a contented sigh. "Don't they make a handsome pair?"

"Handsome, indeed," agreed Olivia diplomatically. "Mrs. Brandemere, I hate to cut short your evening, but may I impose upon your hospitality and beg you to take me home?"

Instantly, Mrs. Brandemere was all concern. "Are you unwell, my dear? I told Lady Hawthorne it would not do. You must take better care of yourself, or—"

"It is not for myself that I ask, but for Miss Hawthorne," interrupted Olivia, cutting short the lecture she knew was about to begin. "Georgina has suddenly taken ill."

"Of course, we must take her home. But—where is she?"

"I—That is, Lord Mannerly very generously agreed to escort her," Olivia improvised rapidly, hoping that, if Georgina were recognized, her explanation might scotch any scandal.

Throughout the drive home, Olivia offered deliberately vague replies to Mrs. Brandemere's inquiries as to the nature and seriousness of Miss Hawthorne's malady. Thankfully, the interrogation did not last long, as Mrs. Brandemere was soon distracted by the plodding pace of a carriage some distance ahead, as well as shocked by the colorful outpourings of a young man driving a hackney carriage.

"Depend upon it, some young pot-valiant who fancies himself a coachman," remarked the offended chaperone in tones of deepest disapproval. "He is indeed fortunate the carriage is blocking his way, or he would have no doubt killed himself by now."

Olivia returned no comment to this observation, too distressed over the fates of her future husband and his sister to be concerned with that of a stranger. At last the carriage set her down in Curzon Street, and she burst through the front door and into the drawing room, expecting to see Sir Harry there in his Lady Hawthorne garb. But the room was empty. Finding the dining room similarly unoccupied, she scurried up the stairs and searched the upstairs rooms, but to no avail: Harry was clearly not at home. Choking back a groan of frustration, she returned to the drawing room and gave the bell pull a tug.

"Coombes," she said when the butler appeared, "where is Lady

Hawthorne?"

"I cannot say, miss," replied the butler. "She summoned a hackney immediately after you left, and has not returned."

"And did he—*she*—say where she was going?"

"No, miss."

"Very well, Coombes," she said with a heavy sigh. "That will be all."

Alone once more, there was nothing Olivia could do but pace the floor and await Sir Harry's return. Perhaps, she thought, he had gone to his club. She knew he was a member of White's, but she could hardly storm that male bastion and demand an audience. No, she could only wait and hope that he would not stay out all night. Back and forth she paced, with the white domino she had forgotten to take off billowing out behind her like a ship in full sail. At last tiring of this unproductive activity, she had just collapsed into a chair when a noise at the front of the house, followed by the sound of voices, startled her from her reverie. She leaped to her feet just as a familiar figure in powdered wig and plumed headdress entered the room, followed by a mousy female of indeterminate age whom Olivia had never seen before. Olivia, however, took no notice of this second arrival, for all her attention was focused on the first.

"Harry! Thank God you've come!" she cried, and without further ado flung her arms about the dowager's neck.

But no welcoming arms enfolded her. Instead, the object of her ardor stiffened in her embrace, and an unfamiliar voice addressed her in stentorian tones.

"Miss Darby, I presume?"

"Oh!" Olivia leaped back, her face flaming. "I beg your pardon. You—you must be Lady Hawthorne."

"Must I be? It seems to me there are quite enough of us already," observed the dowager dryly.

"It was very good of you to come, my lady—"

"Nonsense! Now, where is my good-for-nothing grandson? I vow, I hope Georgina has more sense than her brother!"

"I don't know where Harry has gone, and Georgina—" Olivia took a deep breath. "—Georgina has run off with the marquess of Mannerly."

"Good heavens!" uttered Lady Hawthorne. "Have they gone to Gretna Green?"

"Believe me, ma'am, a Gretna marriage would be a blessing." Olivia recounted the sordid story of the marquess's proposed exchange, including details she had not seen fit to put down on paper. "I can only assume that Georgina somehow discovered his plans, and foolishly substituted herself."

"It would appear that insanity runs in the family—on their mother's side, no doubt. Tell me, Miss Darby, did Mannerly reveal where he intended to take you?"

"No, ma'am. He only said that he would return me after we—afterwards—before I was missed."

"Then he cannot have taken her far. Miss Darby, you and I must first track down Georgina—we shall deal with Harry later. Mildred, you will stay here in case the prodigals return!"

Olivia paused only long enough to exchange her domino for a traveling cloak, then followed Lady Hawthorne to the carriage, which was still laden with the dowager's and her companion's bags. Lady Hawthorne gave instructions to the coachman, then joined Olivia within.

"We shall stop at every inn in the immediate vicinity of Vauxhall," she explained as the carriage lurched forward. "Perhaps by the time we locate Georgina, Harry will have returned. My dear Miss Darby, you seem like a sensible young woman; why on earth would you wish to marry my ramshackle grandson?"

Olivia could think of a thousand reasons, but limited her answer to one. "As you are no doubt aware, my lady, Harry is impulsive to a fault. He needs a woman to take care of him—the more so because he fancies himself awake upon every suit."

"And you are willing to shoulder such a burden?" asked the dowager in some surprise.

"Life could hold no greater happiness," Olivia said simply.

"Well! You are an extraordinary young woman, Miss Darby. I only hope my grandson deserves you."

# 15

Full bravely hast thou fleshed
Thy maiden sword.
WILLIAM SHAKESPEARE, *Henry IV*

Georgina, having fobbed Olivia off with a forged message directing her to a location at the opposite end of the gardens, arrived at the rendezvous well before the appointed hour. Here she divested herself of her gray domino to reveal the white one underneath and, finding nothing else to do with her discarded raiment, stuffed it unceremoniously into the shrubbery.

Lord Mannerly, arriving precisely at twelve, saw the ghostly figure in white and reached his hand inside his own black domino so that he might withdraw his pocket watch. After checking the hour, he replaced his timepiece and bestowed upon his companion a nod of approval.

"You are early, my dear," he said, bowing over her hand. "I could almost flatter myself that you are not so reluctant as you would have me believe."

Georgina offered no reply, but kept her head lowered and her hood drawn forward to conceal what her half-mask could not.

"Then again, perhaps not," continued the marquess, frowning beneath his mask as a fold of white satin fell over his hand. "This is not the domino I ordered from Madame Franchot; she was quite right when she said no other satin could match its texture. Was there something wrong with it, or could you not bring yourself to accept a gift from my hand? Oh, well, it matters not. Shall we go?"

After the slightest of hesitations, Georgina laid her hand on the marquess's proffered arm. She would have to go with him, as it would not do to confront him in the middle of one of London's most popular attractions. Still, it was not until he led her through the gates and handed her into his carriage that Georgina began to know fear.

"Wh—where are we going, sir?" she asked in a whisper, lest he should recognize her voice.

Mannerly's lip curled in a cynical smile as the stone-faced coachman shut the door, sealing them alone together within the dark confines of the carriage. "Did you think I would ravish you in the middle of the pavilion? Give me credit for a little discretion, my dear. We are going to a place where we may be alone, with no questions asked. Afterwards, I shall return you to your chaperone, just as I promised."

Far from putting her at ease, these reassurances only confirmed Georgina's worst suspicions. Yet she dared not reveal herself now, when there was no one nearby who might come to her aid. Why, the marquess might be furious with her, and who knew what he might do in his rage? She shrank back into the corner of the carriage, no longer sure of her ability to show him the error of his ways.

"You need have no fear on my account," said the marquess, observing this maneuver with jaded amusement. "I have no intention of making violent love to you, my dear. Revenge, no matter how satisfying, is never an excuse for a lack of delicacy."

"Revenge?" echoed Georgina, still in a whisper. "But what has O—what have I done to you, that you should desire vengeance?"

"Why, nothing at all. You are merely the lovely pawn by which I shall avenge myself upon your intended bridegroom. Ah," he said as the carriage rolled to a stop. "We have arrived."

A moment later the door was opened. Lord Mannerly disembarked first, then handed his lady down with all due ceremony. Georgina looked about her as well as she might, given the hood obstructing her vision, and discovered that he had brought her to an inn whose carved wooden sign identified it as the Crossed Swords. Recalling the brevity of the journey and the marquess's avowed intention of returning her to Mrs. Brandemere, she judged that the location of this establishment could not be very far from Vauxhall.

Once inside, it became evident that the marquess had put a great deal of advance preparation into his revenge. The taproom was empty, and the innkeeper was nowhere in sight, but Mannerly led his lady unerringly up a steep flight of narrow stairs to a bedchamber where a fire was already burning. Georgina's hackles rose as she noted that the bed was turned down.

Mannerly closed the door and turned the key in the lock, then removed his domino and cast it over the back of a chair. "Now then, my dear," he said, advancing toward Georgina, "shall we get on with it?"

"My lord, there is—something you should know—" she stammered, backing away from him.

"I shall know all I need very shortly," said he, dismissing her concerns. "Come, Miss Darby, a bargain is a bargain."

He plucked at the strings of her domino, and the white satin hood fell away to reveal Georgina Hawthorne, her coppery curls aglow in the firelight.

"Good God!" uttered the marquess.

While her captor was momentarily bereft of speech, Georgina took a deep breath and launched into her prepared sermon. "My lord, I must beg you to reconsider a course of action which you will ultimately live to regret—"

"Have no fear," said Mannerly, cutting short this homily. "I draw the line at kidnapping children fresh from the schoolroom!"

Somehow Georgina found this unflattering assessment even more offensive than all the marquess's other sins combined. "I am not a child, and I have been out of the schoolroom for almost a year!"

"A female Methuselah, in fact," observed the marquess wryly. "At any rate, it would never do for you to be discovered here with me. Put your domino back on, and I will endeavor to return you to Vauxhall without anyone being the wiser."

Georgina should have been vastly pleased to have succeeded in her mission so easily, but instead, she found herself oddly reluctant to end the *tête-à-tête*. "First you must tell me, my lord. What did he do?"

Lord Mannerly had picked up Georgina's domino where it lay on the floor and was in the act of placing it across her shoulders when he froze, baffled by the apparent *non sequitur*. "I beg your pardon?"

"What did Harry do, to make you so thirsty for revenge?"

He knew he should tell her it was not a fit story for a lady's ears, but something about the wide hazel eyes gazing expectantly up at him required an answer.

"It is a long story. As might be expected, it involves a woman."

"Olivia?"

"I said a woman, not a lady."

"Oh," said Georgina, pondering this disclosure with mixed emotions. "And she preferred Harry?"

The marquess winced. "That, my child, is the unkindest cut of all! As a matter of fact, your brother effectively removed me from the lists by the simple expedient of emptying a glass of Madeira over my head."

"Well! I must say, I think that very shabby of him."

"In all fairness to Sir Harry, I do not believe malice was his intent. It was an accident, Miss Hawthorne."

As a new thought occurred to her, Georgina fixed her gaze on the diamond winking in the marquess's immaculate cravat. "If you have gone to such extremes to avenge an accident, my lord, you must—you must have loved her very much."

Mannerly looked nonplussed at the very suggestion. "Loved her? In truth, Miss Hawthorne, I can hardly remember what she looked like. It was the loss of my dignity which I could not allow to go unchallenged."

All Georgina's sympathy for the marquess instantly evaporated. "And you are prepared to ruin Harry—yes, and Olivia too!—because of an imagined blow to your *pride*? Well! I daresay if I had a glass of Madeira at hand, I should be tempted to pour it over you myself!"

This was not at all the response the marquess had expected. "Now, see here, my girl—"

"Oh, I see it all too clearly! You, my lord, are nothing but an arrogant popinjay!"

"Indeed? Then give me leave to inform *you*, miss, that you are a self-righteous hypocrite, and if you intend to wed that vicar of yours, you had best learn to distinguish between play-acting piety and the real thing!"

Thus Selwyn St. George, fifth marquess of Mannerly, indulging in a bout of name-calling with a girl barely out of the schoolroom. Instantly the fire went out of Georgina's flashing eyes, only to be replaced by tears.

"Here, now!" protested the marquess, dismayed. "I should never have said such a thing—I beg your pardon!"

"N-no, no, y-you are quite right," sniffed Georgina. "I—I fear I am not a—a suitable wife for a minister, after all."

Lord Mannerly could not have said why he should find this admission so satisfying, but observing with interest her quivering lower lip and the swift rise and fall of her bosom, he silently conceded that his dismissal of Georgina as a mere schoolgirl, and therefore beneath his notice, was in error. But before he could pursue this novel idea to any sort of a conclusion, a disturbance below recalled his attention to the matter at hand.

"Good heavens!" cried Georgina, similarly distracted. "What is that?"

"That, if I mistake not," said the marquess with a world-weary sigh, "is your rescuer."

Admonishing Georgina to remain out of sight in the bedchamber, Lord Mannerly left the room and descended the staircase to find a very vocal Sir Harry in full evening attire of tailcoat and pantaloons, demanding from the innkeeper the whereabouts of a tall masked gentleman accompanied by a lady in a white domino. The innkeeper, who had been well paid for his silence, was denying all knowledge of any such persons when Mannerly, without ever raising his voice, interrupted his protestations.

"Good evening, Hawthorne," said the marquess smoothly. "How may I be of service to you?"

Sir Harry looked up and beheld his nemesis standing on the stairs. "You have something that belongs to me," he informed the marquess bluntly. "I want it back."

"May I suggest we discuss this in the private parlor, away from inquisitive ears?" Lord Mannerly gestured toward a door leading from the taproom.

Seeing that they were indeed the object of several curious stares, Sir Harry nodded his acquiescence, and led the way to this chamber. Here, too, a fire burned cheerfully in the grate, and over the mantle were hung the two burnished swords from which the hostelry derived its name. Lord Mannerly entered the room in Sir Harry's wake and closed the door behind him.

"All right, Mannerly, where is she?" demanded Sir Harry, eyeing his adversary through narrowed eyes that glittered dangerously.

Lord Mannerly, seeing the intensity in the look being leveled upon him, judged that the violence of feeling in those eyes transcended mere sibling devotion.

"Ah!" he exclaimed as one enlightened. "Am I to understand that you desire the return of the fair Olivia?"

"'Miss Darby,' to you," retorted Sir Harry through clenched teeth.

The marquess shrugged. "As you wish. Unfortunately, I am powerless to assist you. So far as I know, Miss Darby is at Vauxhall Gardens," he added, adhering to the letter of truth if not its spirit.

"Liar!" spat Sir Harry, striding to the fireplace and laying hands on the swords that hung over the mantle. "By God, Mannerly, you have been the thorn in my side just long enough! You will give me satisfaction, sir!"

"I am, of course, yours to command."

Sir Harry tossed one of the swords to the marquess, who caught it by the hilt. Divesting themselves of coats and gloves was the work of a minute, as was joining in the rare cooperative effort of shoving the furniture back against the wall. At last ready to begin, the two combatants faced one another, teasing each other with the tips of their blades, until Sir Harry made the first thrust and the battle was joined in earnest. For the next several minutes there was no sound but the ringing of steel on steel and the labored breathing of the participants. Sir Harry had not the benefit of the French fencing master which the marquess had enjoyed in his younger days, but he had all the advantages of youth and purpose in his favor, and the marquess, parrying his thrusts, was forced to admit a certain grudging respect for his foe.

Georgina, meanwhile, was left alone in the upstairs bedchamber with nothing to do but listen for sounds of any activity from below. Upon hearing her brother's voice, she had forced herself to remain above, trusting Lord Mannerly to settle the matter quietly and return her to Vauxhall—or to her brother—as he had promised. But when the steely clash of swords met her ears, she realized that the interview had taken a very different turn. She hurried down the stairs and followed the sound to the private parlor opening off the public taproom. Finding herself locked out, she pounded on the door, calling first her brother's name and then Mannerly's, but it was doubtful whether the two men, intent upon their duel, ever heard her cries. In desperation, she turned to the innkeeper for assistance.

Although he had been well compensated by the marquess for his silence, that astute businessman reasoned that the shedding of blood upon the new cut-pile Wilton carpet (for which he had just paid all of four shillings the yard) was not reckoned to be part of the bargain. Producing a key from a drawer behind the bar, he inserted it into the keyhole, and a moment later the door was open.

"Gentlemen, please, stop this at once!" beseeched their host.

"Harry, you'll kill him!" shrieked Georgina.

"Well, what the devil do you think he's trying to do to me?" panted Sir Harry, too intent on avoiding the marquess's flashing blade to question his sister's presence in a place where she had no business being.

"Gentlemen, gentlemen—"

"Harry! Lord Mannerly, *please*!"

But the combatants continued to bob, thrust, and parry, paying no attention to the protestations of their audience. Sir Harry's strength was beginning to flag, for he had thrown himself into the battle with reckless abandon, whereas the marquess, some twelve years his senior and aware of the limitations that came with age, had paced himself. Indeed, Sir Harry might shortly have been very much the worse for wear, had it not been for the timely arrival of a new player upon the scene.

"Stop this foolishness at once, or I shall send for the constable!" demanded a booming female voice.

Lord Mannerly darted a quick glance at the newcomer and beheld an elderly lady in an outdated powdered wig. Having been long convinced that "Lady Hawthorne" existed solely in the person of the young man on the other end of his sword, the marquess was so astonished at this sight that, for the merest fraction of a second, he relaxed his guard. Sir Harry, to his own surprise as much as Mannerly's, found his mark, and his point sliced through the marquess's sleeve up the length of his arm, where it buried itself in his shoulder.

As Mannerly's immaculate white linen turned crimson with blood, Georgina broke away from the little group clustered about the door and ran to cling to the marquess's uninjured arm. "Oh, my lord! He has killed you!"

"Nonsense! You overestimate your brother's skill with a sword, my child," panted Mannerly, applying his handkerchief to the wound. "'Tis the merest scratch."

Sir Harry's sword fell from his nerveless hand as he stared open-mouthed at the spectacle of his sister hanging upon the marquess's arm.

"Well, Miss Darby, I can tell you were quite right to send for me," said Lady Hawthorne, surveying the scene with a marked air of disapproval. "Innkeeper, we shall require hot water, and as many sheets as you can spare."

"Yes, my lady, right away!" As his host bustled off to carry out the dowager's orders, Sir Harry came to life.

"Grandmama! And Livvy!" Forgetting his wounded adversary and distraught sister, Sir Harry rapidly crossed the room to seize Olivia by the shoulders. "Livvy, darling, are you all right? I thought Mannerly had you!"

"I am fine," Olivia assured him, clinging to his arms through the thin fabric of his shirt. "I was supposed to have gone with Mannerly, but Georgina somehow found out and—"

"You—would have gone with Mannerly?" Sir Harry echoed bleakly.

"Only for you, Harry. You see, Mannerly found out that you were 'Lady Hawthorne,' and he threatened to expose you unless I agreed to—that is, he offered to exchange—" Breaking off in confusion, she fixed her gaze upon the top button of his waistcoat.

"I should have killed him when I had the chance!" growled Sir Harry, glowering at his fallen adversary, who, having been seated in a chair before the fire, was submitting with every appearance of willingness to Georgina's tender ministrations.

"We shall deal with the marquess shortly," said Lady Hawthorne, cutting her grandson off before he could act on his more bloodthirsty impulses. "For now, I daresay the two of you have much to say to each other. I shall give you five minutes, but no more—you have strained the bounds of propriety quite enough already."

With those words, she herded her granddaughter and Mannerly out of the room, advising the marquess to take himself to one of the bedchambers upstairs before he bled all over the carpet. Having emptied the private parlor of all its occupants but two, she firmly shut the door.

Alone with Olivia at last, Sir Harry had so much to say to her that he didn't know quite where to begin. Of his allotted five minutes, he wasted perhaps ten seconds in stroking his shorn jaw before finding his tongue.

"I don't know what to say, Livvy, except that you made a bad bargain," he said at last. "I'm not worth such a sacrifice."

"I'm sorry about your sidewhiskers, Harry," Olivia answered, blinking back tears. "By deliberately flouting your wishes and encouraging Lord Mannerly, I put you in danger. I shall not easily forgive myself for that."

"You've nothing to forgive yourself for," Sir Harry insisted, possessing himself of her hands. "Livvy, I asked you to marry me once because our parents wished it, and because I wanted a biddable wife who would not interfere with my pleasures. I am asking you now because I find I cannot tolerate the thought of life without you. So for the second time, if you can bring yourself to marry a blind, jealous fool who loves you to distraction, will you do me the honor of becoming my wife?"

Olivia smiled up at him, her eyes sparkling with tears. "Yes, Harry, with all my—"

She got no further, for Sir Harry dragged her into a ruthless embrace which would have bereft her of speech even had she been able to free her lips from his—although it must be noted that she made no visible effort to do so. Instead, she wrapped her arms around him and returned his kiss with every appearance of enthusiasm. Silence reigned in the private parlor for the next four minutes and twenty-four seconds, until at last the door knob rattled and the door opened to reveal Lady Hawthorne standing on the threshold.

"Lud, but this room positively reeks of April and May," she remarked, sailing into the room. "I daresay you spoke scarcely more than a dozen words to each other the entire time."

Sir Harry offered no comment, but devoted his full attention to the adjustment of his cravat, while Olivia was similarly absorbed in replacing the several hairpins which had somehow worked themselves loose from her coiffure. Their seeming fascination with these mundane tasks, as well as their heightened color, was all the proof Lady Hawthorne needed as to the accuracy of her speculation.

"And now," declared the dowager, "if you two are quite finished, we must rejoin your sister and the marquess upstairs."

"You left Georgie alone with that bounder?" demanded Sir Harry, aghast.

"Not at all. I left them under the chaperonage of the innkeeper's wife."

If this set Sir Harry's mind at ease, that agreeable sensation did not last long. Upstairs, the marquess lay in bed propped against the pillows. His torn and bloodied shirt had been removed, and his shoulder bandaged with torn strips of bedsheets. The innkeeper's wife sat complacently in one corner of the room, while Georgina had pulled a chair alongside the bed, from which location she attempted to spoon-feed the invalid from a bowl of broth.

"So you will survive, I see," remarked Sir Harry as he entered the room. "More's the pity."

"I regret that I cannot oblige you by dying just yet," returned the marquess, putting his nurse gently aside so that he might rise from his bed of suffering to confront his erstwhile foe. "Hawthorne, I trust you will sympathize with my plight. After having failed in my attempt to seduce your fiancée, I now find myself in the deucedly awkward position of having to ask your permission to pay my addresses to your sister."

This pronouncement had a profound effect on both Hawthorne siblings.

"The devil, you say!" sputtered Sir Harry. "Why, if I hadn't already pinked you once, I would—"

"No!" cried Georgina, her face white with shock. "My lord, you must not!"

Lord Mannerly looked at her with an expression approaching tenderness. "My poor child, if word of this night's work gets out, do you truly think your vicar will still wish to marry you?"

"Pray, sir, do not think that you must marry me to—to salvage my reputation, or some such thing—"

"My good girl, I have never felt myself obliged to salvage any woman's reputation. If you truly think I would offer you marriage for such a jingle-brained reason as that, you are even greener than I first supposed!"

"Oh," said Georgina, quite cowed.

"Georgina is far too young to marry anyone, as her behavior thus far proves," insisted her brother.

To Sir Harry's surprise, Lord Mannerly did not attempt to dispute this statement. "Then we shall wait until the end of the Season before making any sort of announcement. That will give me a month or better to court her in earnest."

"A month? Not even in a year, Mannerly!"

"Tell me, Sir Harry, do you plan to wait a year or more to wed Miss Darby?"

Sir Harry cast a look of comic dismay at his intended. "Only if she insists!"

"Then you will understand my reluctance to agree to your terms. Shall we split the difference and say six months?"

The marquess held out his left hand (his right being, at the moment, out of commission), and after a moment of severe inner struggle, Sir Harry took it.

"Very wise," said Lady Hawthorne, observing this exchange. "Best to accept it with as good a grace as possible. Lord Mannerly appears to me to be the sort of man who gets what he wants."

"Not always," replied Sir Harry with a secret smile for Olivia. "But what about the vicar, Georgie? I thought you wanted to marry *him*!"

"I have decided that Mr. Collier and I would not suit," Georgina replied primly.

"Well, you would have made him miserable," said Sir Harry with brotherly candor. "Of course, you'll probably make Mannerly miserable, too, but at least I shall have the satisfaction of knowing that he deserves to be so."

"It is unfortunate that Lord Mannerly's attentions to Miss Darby were so very marked," observed Lady Hawthorne. "Still, six months will at least allow time for the talk to die down, and we shall put it about that the marquess applied to Miss Darby for assistance in fixing his interest with Georgina."

This suggestion found favor with everyone except he whom it most nearly concerned.

"My good woman, I have never found it necessary to apply to a third party for assistance with my, er, *affaires de coeur*!"

"No, I suppose not," returned the dowager. "Therefore, the indignity of being *believed* to have done so will serve as fitting punishment for your part in tonight's escapade. Now, I think it best that you, Mannerly, remain here for the night. Harry will send word to your valet to join you here. As for you, Georgina, make your farewells to his lordship. Harry, you may escort us back to Curzon Street, then take yourself off to your own lodgings and act as if you have been in residence there for the past month!"

ᘓ

It was a weary little group that arrived back in Curzon Street. A dreamy-eyed Georgina bade her grandmother goodnight and floated up the stairs. Olivia, for her part, wanted to spend every possible minute with Sir Harry, and to this end insisted that she felt fine. It was not until this threesome settled in the drawing room for a lengthy conference that Sir Harry noticed that his intended bride's eyelids were starting to droop. Consequently, he ordered her to take herself to bed and, when she showed signs of refusing, threatened to toss her over his shoulder and carry her there himself.

"I think I liked you better as Lady Hawthorne," Olivia complained, softening the blow to Sir Harry's manhood by taking his arm as he walked with her to the foot of the stairs. Here she turned and regarded her betrothed with an earnest expression. "Harry, try not to mind too much about Georgina and Lord Mannerly. I know it is not what you would wish for her, but I think he does care for her, in his own way. Besides, we stand in his debt, you and I."

Sir Harry pondered this idea distastefully. "Much as it galls me to be indebted to Mannerly, I suppose you are right. My God, Livvy, when I think how close we came to making a cold, loveless marriage—"

"No, Harry, never that." She paused long enough to yawn, and Sir Harry, reminded of the lateness of the hour, repeated his demand that she go to bed.

She took two steps before turning back, delaying the inevitable parting as long as possible. "Will you call on us tomorrow?"

Sir Harry snatched her hand from the rail and planted a kiss on it. "Try to keep me away!" he retorted, smiling at Olivia in a way that warmed her all the way down to her toes.

He watched until she disappeared at the landing, then rejoined his grandmother in the drawing room.

"Well, Harry, you've much to explain," remarked the dowager as her grandson collapsed wearily onto a chair.

"And much for which to beg your pardon. Believe me, Grandmama, if I had known how much trouble it would cause, I would never—" He broke off, considering how it had all worked out. Would he have done it anyway?

"Nonsense, my boy, if you had the chance, you would do it again tomorrow."

"Grandmama, you are a mind-reader. Still, there are a few things you should know, and for which I am profoundly sorry. While living here under your name, I was obliged to bring my valet, and to disguise him as a lady's maid, only his disguise was not very good, and—well, the long and short of it is that everyone belowstairs believes you to be keeping a lover!"

Lady Hawthorne was incredulous. "At my age? Surely you jest!"

"Wait, there's more. At one point I found it necessary to speak to my friend, Mr. Wrexham, in private, and when he was ushered to my bedchamber, I'm afraid the footman assumed the worst. And then there was Colonel Gubbins, whom I was obliged to wallop with my reticule when he tried to kiss me. In short, ma'am, I've made a regular mull of your life, and am more than happy to turn it back over to you. Olivia's mother is expected to return to London tomorrow—today, rather—and as soon as she arrives, I should be pleased to escort you back to Bath."

"What humbug!" scoffed Lady Hawthorne. "You know quite well you should be pleased to do no such thing! You would much prefer to remain here in London, dancing attendance on your Miss Darby."

Sir Harry, grinning broadly, made no attempt to refute this statement.

"As for my returning to Bath," replied the dowager with great deliberation, "my London come-out was not a success. By the time your grandfather offered for me, I was twenty-four years old and all but on the shelf, and all the tabbies had it that although I was the daughter of a viscount, I had to content myself with a mere baronet. Now, many years later, I have returned to find myself reputed to be keeping no less than three lovers in my pocket." Lady Hawthorne's face lit up in a mischievous grin. "My dear boy, why on earth would I want to leave *now*?"

# Epilogue

Let all thy joys be as the month of May,
And all thy days be as a marriage day.
FRANCIS QUARLES, *To a Bride*

On a mild sunny day in late September, the Reverend James Collier stood in his pulpit, reading aloud the marriage ceremony from the Book of Common Prayer. The bridal couple stood before him, gorgeously arrayed in their wedding finery: Sir Harry Hawthorne handsome and elegant in a dark blue coat and white waistcoat over black pantaloons, Miss Olivia Darby radiantly beautiful in white India muslin, her dark hair crowned with a wreath of white roses which had been delivered to Darby House just that morning from Sir Harry's own hothouses.

Alas, the vicar's own nuptials were not to be, for Miss Georgina Hawthorne had indeed fallen prey to the temptations of the Metropolis. Glancing at that young lady, who was on this occasion serving her future sister as bridesmaid, Mr. Collier felt a pang of regret. She was very lovely, with her coppery curls tied up with peach-colored ribbons to match her gown.

But there would be time for repining later. For now, those parts of the little parish church not filled with flowers were overflowing with wedding guests, and in addition to his regular parishioners, the good reverend was pleased to see such distinguished visitors as Lord and Lady Clairmont, the bride's sister and brother-in-law; the dowager Lady Hawthorne, who needed no introduction to be instantly recognized as the bridegroom's grandmother; and the marquess of Mannerly, who had driven up from London just the day before.

While Sir Harry Hawthorne repeated the vows that would unite him with Miss Darby, the vicar took the opportunity to study this noble guest. He knew not quite what to make of the marquess's presence. When he had called at Hawthorne Grange the day before with some last-minute inquiries regarding the ceremony, it had seemed to him that Sir Harry regarded his houseguest with thinly veiled hostility. Ordinarily, Mr. Collier would have judged the marquess as the sort of gentleman whom he, as a man of the cloth, could not quite like, yet even he had been disconcerted by Sir Harry's obvious resentment of his visitor. Indeed, he had felt it his Christian duty to do what he might to pour oil on the troubled waters. Yet when he had attempted to apologize to the marquess for his host's abrupt manner, ascribing Sir Harry's lack of civility to premarital sensibilities, the nobleman had come to that pugnacious young man's defense, giving Mr. Collier a blistering set-down for his pains. He could only suppose that Sir Harry and his guest did not despise one another as much as they pretended, and had wisely refrained from interfering again where his assistance was clearly not wanted.

The sounds of Mrs. Darby sniffing audibly into her thoroughly saturated handkerchief recalled the vicar to a sense of his duties and, turning to Olivia, he charged her to repeat the vows just spoken by her intended husband. As Olivia promised to love, honor, and obey, Mr. Collier's thoughts again strayed to Miss Hawthorne, allowing himself one moment to regret that he would never hear those words upon her lips. Glancing down at the young lady who would never be his, he was shocked and disturbed to see her and Lord Mannerly exchanging furtive glances which could only be described as amorous. Merciful heavens! Was that why she had cried off so abruptly? If Miss Hawthorne had succumbed to the worldly charms of the marquess, clearly she was unsuited to be the wife of one in Holy Orders.

Amid the bride's mother's tears, the groom's mother's smiles, and the approving nods of the dowager Lady Hawthorne, he uttered the pronouncement that joined Sir Harry and his lady in holy matrimony, all the while silently thanking his Maker for his narrow escape.

## About the Author

Sheri Cobb South is the author of five popular young adult novels, as well as a number of short stories in various genres including mystery, young adult, and inspirational. Her first love has always been the Regency, however, and in 1996 she won the Royal Ascot Award for *Miss Darby's Duenna*. She is currently working on a sequel to her debut Regency novel, *The Weaver Takes a Wife*.

Sheri lives near Mobile, Alabama with her husband and two children. You may send her e-mail at Cobbsouth@aol.com, or write to her c/o PrinnyWorld Press, P. O. Box 248, Saraland, AL 36571.

**Turn the page for a special preview of**

# Brighton Honeymoon

**coming Summer 2000 from PrinnyWorld Press!**

In this sequel to the highly acclaimed *The Weaver Takes a Wife*, mismatched newlyweds Ethan and Lady Helen Brundy journey to the seaside resort of Brighton for a belated wedding trip—and find themselves with a honeymoon cottage full of guests, including a disapproving dowager, a young woman claiming to be Mr. Brundy's sister, and a skeptical dandy determined to expose her as a fraud.

Ah, Miss Crump," said Sir Aubrey as Polly entered the breakfast room, dressed for the day in a morning gown of figured muslin. "I trust your rest was undisturbed?"

Polly studied her inquisitor through blue eyes clouded with suspicion. If Sir Aubrey was no less handsome than he had appeared the previous day, neither was he any less dangerous.

"What, pray, would have disturbed it?" she asked warily.

Sir Aubrey gave a negligent shrug and applied himself to the task of spreading marmalade on a slice of toast. "Any number of things: indigestion, perhaps, or a guilty conscience—"

"Of what are you accusing me, sir, that it should prevent my sleeping soundly?" inquired Polly in dulcet tones.

Sir Aubrey's expression was all wounded innocence. "Why, nothing, nothing at all! I would no more cast aspersions on the state of your conscience than I would the contents of your stomach—although I must say that if you continue to slather butter all over your bread at that rate, you will find yourself fat as a flawn by middle age."

As Polly stared down at the slice of toast in her hand (which she had unconsciously been covering with butter ever since Sir Aubrey had first begun his interrogation), Lady Tabor took a hand.

"If this is what passes for gallantry these days, Aubrey, I am thankful to be too old for flirtations!"

"As always, Mama, you are quite right. Miss Crump, permit me to redeem myself in my mother's eyes. Your radiant appearance informs me that your repose could not have been other than blissful."

As this declaration was delivered in accents too exaggerated to allow for their being taken at face value, Polly had no illusions as to the speaker's sincerity.

"You are too kind, sir," she responded in like manner. "But any radiance in my appearance must be credited to the beautiful gowns with which Lady Helen has been generous enough to provide me."

"To be sure, Lady Helen has always had exceptional taste," pronounced Lady Tabor.

"Why, thank you," put in Mr. Brundy, bestowing a gratified smile upon the dowager. "And 'ere I was, thinking you didn't like me above 'alf!"

"No doubt her taste in husbands would have been equally nice, had she been at liberty to exercise it," muttered Lady Tabor, glaring at her host.

Silencing her grinning husband with a glance, Lady Helen applied herself to the task of soothing the affronted widow. "Now that Miss Crump has a suitable wardrobe for going about in Society, I have promised to take her to the theater tonight, Lady Tabor. Do say you and Sir Aubrey will give us the pleasure of your company!"

"Will *he* be there?" asked her ladyship, and Lady Helen had no trouble identifying her husband as the object of Lady Tabor's inquiry.

"Mr. Brundy will, of course, escort us," she admitted.

Whatever Lady Tabor's retort might have been, it was cut short by her son. "I am sure I speak for my mother when I say we would be delighted to join you," said Sir Aubrey. "But I should be even more delighted, Miss Crump, if you will first do me the honor of going for a drive with me in my phaeton."

For some reason she could not name, Polly found Sir Aubrey's gallantries even more disturbing than his veiled insinuations.

Nevertheless, with no less than four people awaiting her answer, she could make only one response.

"Thank you, Sir Aubrey, I should be pleased to go driving with you," she said, then rose to refill her coffee cup at the sideboard.

Sir Aubrey, in the meantime, had turned back to his hostess. "Tell me, Lady Helen, what other plans have you made for Miss Crump's amusement?"

"Well, besides the theater, there are the assemblies—dances, Miss Crump, which I am persuaded you will enjoy above all things!—and perhaps we might have a picnic on the beach one day, weather permitting."

"And have you heard of any masquerades being planned?"

Since masked balls were known to promote licentiousness and a familiarity of manner which was not at all the thing, Lady Helen was more than a little taken aback by Sir Aubrey's query. "Masquerades, Sir Aubrey? None that I am aware of. Why do you ask?"

His shrug was a study in well-bred indolence. "No particular reason. Only that I find masquerades fascinating, do not you, Miss Crump? No one is what they appear to be."

From her position at the sideboard, Polly bent a sharp look upon Sir Aubrey, but met only a blank gray gaze. "Why, you are in need of more coffee, sir," she exclaimed, seizing upon the excuse offered by his empty cup. "Pray allow me to let you have it."

And so saying, she emptied the contents of the pot onto Sir Aubrey's lap.

§ § §

**Watch for BRIGHTON HONEYMOON, coming Summer 2000!**

# The Weaver Takes a Wife
## by
## Sheri Cobb South

Haughty Lady Helen Radney is the daughter of a duke and one of London's most beautiful women, but when her father gambles away his fortune, he must marry her off to a rich man—*any* rich man—if he hopes to salvage the family finances.

Enter Mr. Ethan Brundy, once an illegitimate workhouse orphan, now the wealthy owner of a Lancashire cotton mill. He wins her hand through economic necessity. But can this commonest of commoners ever hope to win the heart of his aristocratic bride?

§ § §

**"A truly lovely story...an original twist on the old Pygmalion tale. I fell for the completely unpolished, wholly decent Ethan Brundy, and wouldn't want him any other way."**

**—Emma Jensen, author of *Best Laid Schemes***

§ § §

**"Halfway through reading *The Weaver Takes a Wife,* I was tempted to stop and look again at the copyright notice, just to assure myself that I wasn't reading a long-lost and recently rediscovered work of Georgette Heyer's. This was a delightful read from start to finish...a diamond that shines among the pearls!"**

**—All About Romance**

§ § §

Ask your local bookseller, or use the convenient order form at the back of this book.